EVERNIGHT UNLEASHED

A RAVENWOOD COVEN NOVEL

CARRIE ANN RYAN

EVERNIGHT UNLEASHED

A Ravenwood Coven Novel
By Carrie Ann Ryan

Evernight Unleashed
A Ravenwood Coven Novel
By: Carrie Ann Ryan
© 2021 Carrie Ann Ryan
eBook ISBN: 978-1-950443-70-3
Paperback ISBN: 978-1-950443-71-0

Cover Art by Sweet N Spicy Designs

For Corinne and Jessica.
Thank you for dealing with my version of magic daily.

PRAISE FOR CARRIE ANN RYAN

"Count on Carrie Ann Ryan for emotional, sexy, character driven stories that capture your heart!" – Carly Phillips, NY Times bestselling author

"Carrie Ann Ryan's romances are my newest addiction! The emotion in her books captures me from the very beginning. The hope and healing hold me close until the end. These love stories will simply sweep you away." ~ NYT Bestselling Author Deveny Perry

"Carrie Ann Ryan writes the perfect balance of sweet and heat ensuring every story feeds the soul." - Audrey Carlan, #1 New York Times Bestselling Author

"Carrie Ann Ryan never fails to draw readers in with passion, raw sensuality, and characters that pop off the page. Any book by Carrie Ann is an absolute treat." – New York Times Bestselling Author J. Kenner

"Carrie Ann Ryan knows how to pull your heartstrings and make your pulse pound! Her wonderful Redwood Pack series will draw you in and keep you reading long into the night. I can't wait to see what comes next with the new generation, the Talons. Keep them coming, Carrie Ann!" –Lara Adrian, New York Times bestselling author of CRAVE THE NIGHT

"With snarky humor, sizzling love scenes, and brilliant, imaginative worldbuilding, The Dante's Circle series reads as if Carrie Ann Ryan peeked at my personal wish list!" – NYT Bestselling Author, Larissa Ione

"Carrie Ann Ryan writes sexy shifters in a world full of passionate happily-ever-afters." – *New York Times* Bestselling Author Vivian Arend

"Carrie Ann's books are sexy with characters you can't help but love from page one. They are heat and heart blended to perfection." *New York Times* Bestselling Author Jayne Rylon

Carrie Ann Ryan's books are wickedly funny and deliciously hot, with plenty of twists to keep you guessing. They'll keep you up all night!" USA Today Bestselling Author Cari Quinn

"Once again, Carrie Ann Ryan knocks the Dante's Circle series out of the park. The queen of hot, sexy, enthralling paranormal romance, Carrie Ann is an author not to miss!" *New York Times* bestselling Author Marie Harte

EVERNIGHT UNLEASHED

In the dramatic conclusion to the Ravenwood Coven series by NYT Bestselling Author Carrie Ann Ryan, this sleeping magical paranormal town knows that war can be a beginning...and an ending.

Rowen Ravenwood is the final witch of her line—the only one standing in the way of Oriel, the dark necromancer who wants the core of the town's magic for his own. With each passing battle and loss, Rowen is one step closer to losing it all if she doesn't rely on the one man she refuses to love again. Only this time she might not have a choice when family secrets come to light.

Ash Christopher's family curse hit him harder than anyone knows. He's cool, relentless, and only feels what he needs to in order to survive. He's gained everything in power and lost all else to his ambition—including Rowen.

After all, a man cannot have a soul mate when he does not possess a soul.

The town of Ravenwood is dying and as the final battles come to pass, it will take the courage of a coven reborn, a mating bond broken, and a love worth fighting for in order to save all before it is lost.

Ash

B*efore*

ROWEN WAS MY FOREVER.

The starlight danced across her face; her eyes bright as the magic flowed between us. I could barely keep up with the energy whirling within her, and that was saying something. The earth magic cascading along my skin sunk to my soul, and I held out my hands. The air blew through Rowen's hair, the dark strands floating, as if flying. She was gorgeous, in her element, and not just within the magic.

This was who she was meant to be, and I was just grateful that she allowed me to be here. That I loved the woman in front of me with every ounce of my being.

"Are you ready?" Rowen asked, her voice soft.

"Always," I whispered.

She opened her mouth, the magic sparking between us as we began the spell.

"As we walk from the past and into the future,

Know we are the observers and those who push through to the new season.

Bring forth new life, new hopes, and new choices,

Walk away from the past that haunts,

And towards the future that brings forth the goddess and light.

May we walk into the new season and life.

So mote it be."

Warmth infused over the two of us, and I grinned, leaning down to press my lips against hers. She had sharp features, a strong jaw, and catlike eyes that were deep pools of gray that always pulled me in no matter what she was doing.

I leaned down, picked up her wrist, and pressed my lips to the Ravenwood symbol etched on her skin. She had gotten the tattoo before she had turned eighteen when her aunt hadn't been looking.

I had just smiled and had gotten a similar one on my chest.

I wore the Ravenwood line on my body, though I

wasn't a Ravenwood. I was a Christopher—one of the three founding families of our little town in Pennsylvania.

Magic infused the area, and those who were its residents knew of witches, shifters, fae, and other magics. And it was the strength of our bonds as the coven that kept the secrets intact and kept us safe. Rowen was the last of her line now, the last Ravenwood witch. Though I knew she still grieved for her family, she was strength personified and was ready to protect her people, no matter what. And it was my job to protect her.

Rowen reached out and traced the Ravenwood marking, the symbol of our coven along my chest. "I do appreciate you doing this spell with me while you're shirtless. It's given me a wonderful focal point."

I rolled my eyes and she leaned forward and kissed the pentagram on my forearm. I shook my head and kissed her again, pushing her backward. She let out a small laugh, and I bit her lip before sliding my fingers between her legs. She groaned, and I hiked up her skirt slightly so I could have better access. She was warm, wet, and all mine.

She gave me a sleepy and content smile, like a cat in cream. "Is it the magic that's making you like this? Or something more?"

"You always make me like this, Rowen," I groaned softly before I took her lips again, delving my fingers between her wet folds. She groaned, spreading her thighs for me, and I settled in between them, pressing kisses to her skin and then over the pentagram on her inner thigh that was just for me—no one else.

"I'm going to say that I'm glad that you used magic for this tattoo because I'd have to kill the person who did this for you."

She slid her hands through my hair and moaned. "Possessive much?"

"I'm always possessive with you, Rowen. That's the problem."

I nestled between her thighs, slid her panties to the side fully, and licked. She arched against me, her thighs going around my shoulders as I began to kiss her intimately. I spread her folds, needing her, wanting her taste. The magic settled around us like fireflies buzzing in the air. She was air, and I was earth. She was our coven leader, and I was her servant, always.

I pulled her dress up higher, and she leaned forward to tug it over her head. She laid nearly naked now in the grass, the trees shielding us from others, the magic between us making sure this moment was private behind her ancestral home.

Her anchor, dandelion seeds blowing across her shoulders and body, moved in a wind tunnel around her skin, tickling my own as I continued to lap at her.

My anchor, a full redwood forest of ink, pulsated along my body. I had full-sleeve tattoos, the same forest up my back and down my thighs. With each passing month for the past year, another tree would spout, and my magic would grow stronger. It wasn't unheard of for powerful witches, but it was surprising. Only I couldn't care too much about that in this moment.

I continued to lap up her spicy scent, and when she came magic shook the air, and I sat up between her legs, needing her taste, needing her everything.

"Ash," she whispered.

I leaned forward, slid my hands over those sinful curves of hers, and kissed her.

She hummed along me, her thighs now pressing against my hips. And when she magic-ed my pants away with just a quick spell under her breath, we laughed. So, I rolled to my back, let her straddle me, and let her take control. She was my priestess, after all, my everything. And then she met my gaze and slid over my length. I groaned, her wetness tight and hot around me. She rubbed against me, her hips rocking slightly as I gripped her sides and continued to move in and out of her. Her mouth parted, and I looked up at her and knew she was mine.

We may only be eighteen, young in the eyes of some, coven leaders in the eyes of others, but I didn't care.

This was the woman that I would marry, the woman I would bond with.

The woman that would break the Christopher curse, no matter what the curse became. We knew what had happened to each of my family members with our curse, but we didn't know mine yet. But I knew with

Rowen at my side, we could survive anything. Any curse, any coming darkness that the prophecies told us about.

With Rowen at my side, we could be anyone and be anything.

She leaned down, her breasts in my face, so I sucked a rosy nipple into my mouth. "Ash," she murmured.

"Come for me, come on me, Rowen. One more time."

"Always. For you."

And she came, her body blushing beautifully, and I slid my hands around the back of her neck, pulling her closer to me, as I filled her, both of us letting our magic wrap around one another. And then it clicked, a bond so old and perfect that I could barely breathe.

This was happiness. This was truth. My soul sung for her.

Rowen's eyes widened as she looked down at me, and we grinned, the mating bond snapping into place between both of us as if it had always been there, waiting for this moment in time. This wasn't the first time we had been together, but this was the first time it felt like this was our forever.

Tears slid down her cheeks, and I wiped them away, kissing her slowly as my soul wrapped around hers, and hers did the same to mine.

"It's true. You're mine." I sat up, my body still shaking from release, my cock buried deep in her. I wrapped my arms around her. "I love you."

"I love you so much, Ash. I can't believe I'm this happy."

She smiled wide, looking as if she had the whole world ahead of her, and she did. We did. Together. And so, I kissed her harder, the bond between us radiating with hope, a future, and love. I didn't even sound like myself, but I fucking loved this.

We made love again, and then we dressed, thankfully Rowen magic-ing back my pants. And as our fingers tangled, I kissed the top of her head and led her home.

"I need to meet the triplets and Jaxton. I promised them we'd go over a few things. You okay?"

"Of course, I'm okay. I'll see you soon?" She looked so innocent, as if scared everything was going to change. And hell, it would, but then again, I didn't mind.

We would be starting college soon, but we would all be going together. Rowen and I would be going to the university right outside Ravenwood, making the drive for it was going to be difficult, but we had known what was going to happen when we had signed up for school. We needed classes, needed our degrees to begin our human lives, all the while connecting ourselves to the paranormal ones that lay in Ravenwood. Countless founding families had done it before us, and we would do it again.

Together.

I kissed her one more time, needing her, and then I left her standing on her porch, her air magic billowing her hair, her smile wide, her eyes knowing. She wore a dress of dark gray that flowed in the breeze, and she looked like my goddess. My witch.

And I loved her with every ounce of my being.

I rubbed my fist over the Ravenwood symbol over my chest, wondering why it burned slightly. Maybe we had used too much magic during our coupling and the spell itself. I shook my head and walked towards where the bears slumbered. I grinned, thinking of the bear triplets, and how Trace and I had a few plans later that day to surprise my sister. I shook my head and stumbled, confused as to where the dizziness had come from.

I scratched at my chest, wondering what the hell was going on. I opened my mouth and tried to scream, but nothing came out.

Instead, a numbness began to settle over me, beginning at my fingertips, slowly creeping up my skin, as if I could see the layering of something coming, something stretching me.

I tried to breathe, tried to do anything, but there was nothing. I sat on my knees, my hands digging into the dirt as I sucked in lungfuls of air, trying to catch my breath.

Something was wrong.

The pentagram on my forearm pulsed, as did the Ravenwood symbol on my chest. More trees bursts along my arms. It was intensifying, as if my magic was increasing, and yet I couldn't feel anything. There was nothing.

I fell to the side, my hands over my chest as I shook, my mouth going dry, bile rising up my throat.

And then I *knew*…because there was nothing else.

There was no connection, no bond, no need for the warmth that I had left behind. No need for wondering what that warmth can be.

I scrambled up, the last vestiges of who I was left behind with each passing step. I made my way to the home I shared with Laurel and staggered upstairs, ignoring the shout from my little sister.

I met my gaze in the reflection of the mirror in my bathroom, at the blue eyes that had once been dark pools but now were shattered with gray and silver, and *I knew.*

The Christopher curse had taken something from me. Just like it was taking Laurel from us.

And yet, I couldn't care.

After all, I had no soul.

I was no longer here. No longer anyone.

Some part of me screamed, begging for whoever looked in the mirror to stop it. To fight. To push against whatever was breaking and fight harder.

But there was nothing.

There could be nothing.

Trace, Laurel, and Jaxton stood in the doorway behind me, their eyes wide.

"What happened?" my little sister asked.

I let out a breath. "Nothing. Nothing's happened. Go. Go make your decision between the two and leave me the fuck alone."

I heard the words coming out of my mouth. They were cruel, callous. This wasn't me.

Stop it. Fight for yourself. Don't be a dick. Tell them. Tell them you've lost your soul. They need to know. They need to find a way to get it back. We can't protect Ravenwood. We can't protect Laurel. We cannot protect Rowen without our soul. Fight for that bond. Why are you not fighting?

I pushed away the little voice in my head, the screaming.

It didn't matter. It couldn't.

Others were shouting at me, but I pushed my way through them, using the force of my magic against my friends and family. They fell against the wall, their eyes wide as they pulled themselves up, reaching for me. But I flipped them off as if they were flies.

I didn't need them. I didn't need anybody.

Why couldn't they see that? Why couldn't they see I didn't need the prophecy, or this town, or this coven?

I was the final remaining male witch of this town. I was the power.

I needed no one.

I stepped outside, intending to make my way to my car and to get out of the dregs of this town.

And Rowen stood there. Her chest heaved as if she had been running, and tears slid down her cheeks.

"Ash, what's wrong? Why can't I feel you? What happened to the bond?"

I tilted my head as I looked at her. Part of me

screamed, and the other part of me knew I was crueler than I would ever be in my life.

But it needed to be like this.

Didn't she understand? It needed to be like this.

"I'm leaving. Leaving this town, this coven. I intend to make something of myself. And I don't need Ravenwood to make it happen."

Others were shouting, as was the voice in my head, but once again I ignored it.

"Ash. You can't be saying this." She moved forward, but I stepped back out of her way, angling towards my vehicle.

"Goodbye. I mean, it was nice and all, but, as you can see, I'm going to do just fine without you and this town. Grow up, Rowen. Be the little witch you're meant to be."

She slapped me, her hand leaving a sting behind—the first moment of feeling I had had in the past hour. "You bastard. What is going on?"

"The curse," my little sister called from behind me. "It's the curse, Rowen."

Rowen turned to Laurel and then back at me, her eyes wide and filling with tears. "No. Ash. Fight it. Fight for everything. We can do this. We can bring your soul back, I promise."

I tilted my head and stared at her before I smiled. And it was a cruel smile, one I knew I would never use again because I couldn't. Because that screaming voice in my head, though I was deafening it, would never let me do this again.

"Why would I fight? Who would I fight for? Oh, Rowen, you can't be my soulmate. After all, how can you have a soulmate without a soul?"

And then I walked away from her as she fell to her knees and broke down, the others comforting her. But nobody came for me. And nobody would.

Because I was a Christopher, not a Ravenwood.

And I had to find my own path.

One without a curse, without a town, and without magic.

And yet the screaming part of myself, even through its silence, begged.

But I ignored it.

After all, it was the only way for me to live.

Even if I knew that this was only the beginning.

CHAPTER

TWO

Rowen

Present Day

I LOVED MY TOWN. There was nothing better than a fall day in Ravenwood, Pennsylvania. Where wind blew through the trees, the bright reds, golds, oranges, and yellows of the tall trees billowing with each passing breeze. The leaves fell in swirls of color and emotion, and I held up my face to the air, letting the magic that was the town of Ravenwood seep into my bones and gently caress my skin.

I let my magic sizzle slightly, the wind calling to me. I stood on Main Street as passersby smiled at me or moved around me. I wasn't standing in the middle of the sidewalk, but as our town was old, the sidewalks weren't meant for more than two people or so at a time in some places, so one inevitably bumped into another human, shifter, or something in between.

The leaves fell, the coming of autumn pungent in the air.

This was my time, one where my magic was not solely harnessed within death and destruction or rebirth and promise. But of change, and what could be. My anchor danced around my body, the seeds of the dandelion tickling my sides as a small smile played at my face.

Each anchor represented the element that a witch held. For a shifter, it was of that animal—not another soul, but a part that connected you to the magic that was that aspect of yourself. I wasn't sure what the fae held in terms of an anchor because I had never seen one unclothed.

A smile played on my lips as I opened my eyes and walked towards my magical tourist shop. I would have to ask Jaxton's sister, Nelle, about what anchors the fae held. After all, she was mated to one.

My smile fell, emotion slamming into me as I remembered the paleness on Nelle's face, the mermaid no longer smiling when she had died for those brief moments in the fae king's arms. Our enemy had slain her, and yet, Nelle still lived. Perhaps she wasn't quite who she had once been, she was here and learning to become who she now was. Though, after the ravages of battle and war, were any of us the same person we had once been?

Nelle was alive and breathing and coming to terms with the mating bond with the king of the fae, Aspen. I wasn't sure exactly what she felt or how she was coping. She spent most of her time either in the mer realm below the surface of the sea, or within the limits of the fae territory. The fae were on the outskirts of Ravenwood, but they were still considered part of our town. The same as many of the shifter dwellings that weren't directly in the town limits. The wards that connected me to Ravenwood and the core of our power still protected them. And it was their magic that kept their people far more secure than I ever could on my own.

However, the ward surrounding the town was something that I had been focused on since I had first learned how to strengthen my magic. Long before the coven of three had become who it was, long before I had found out who the darkness was and who our enemy could be. I might not know his face, but I knew his name.

Oriel.

A necromancer, a dark witch, and one who wanted the core power of Ravenwood.

My wards were now strong enough to protect the town without killing me, for now. At least that was what I hoped.

The bells rang above the door as I walked inside my shop and smiled over at my lone worker for the day. Esmeralda grinned and began talking to a mundane tourist, someone without magical talent and one who didn't know of the magics below the surface.

Ravenwood, Pennsylvania, was special. Those who lived within town limits and grew up knowing exactly what was special about our town, knew of magic. They could see beneath the glamours of the fae, knew of the power of witches and the coven. They knew of shifters and could see the bear shifters, and the few wolves, walk around town in their animal form. The stronger the wards were, the more freedom our shifters had. With the coven of three—me, Laurel, and Sage—we were able to bring forth stronger magic, and therefore our glamours were able to hide bear shifters in bear form, walking down a sidewalk next to a human that had no idea who was nearby.

It was part of the quirkiness and core of Ravenwood. It was what we were fighting to the death for—that and the magic beneath our feet that could destroy the world if held in the wrong hands.

"Have a blessed day," Esmeralda said softly to the two women who giggled on their way out.

I smiled at them as well, and they ducked their heads, blushing before they scurried out and piled into the small compact car parallel-parked in front of my store.

I turned and raised a brow at Esmeralda, and she

laughed, her eyebrow ring glistening underneath the overhead light. "Let me guess. They're looking for stones and crystals to help them get through some form of breakup?"

"Yes, they asked for potions, but I didn't think that would be something you would approve of."

I nodded and glanced around the crystal area, noting what was missing. Nothing for love, but for protection, and strength, and for seeing through the darkness. I nodded in approval at Esmeralda as I went behind the antique desk that served as a register.

"Good on you, and no, no special spells to get through love and heartache."

Esmeralda cackled, her smile wide. "It's never worked before, and there's always some form of disaster waiting for you in the end if you do so. Like a broken mirror or a bad perm."

I snorted and went through receipts as Esmeralda went to a box beside her and began unpacking our inventory. Esmeralda was a witch, but she wasn't of the coven. Her blood was diluted enough that she barely held any power but could still feel things through some crystals. She trained with me weekly to focus that power. She couldn't call to an element, couldn't go through most rituals and spells, but she was still a witch.

However, because she didn't have the strength required to keep the wards around Ravenwood secure, her soul wasn't irrevocably tied to that of Ravenwood like mine was.

The center of my chest burned slightly, and I frowned, wondering why that wouldn't desist. I hadn't even realized I had fisted my hand over my chest until Esmeralda gave me a look. "The wards too much again?"

I shook my head, letting my hand fall. Instead, I reached around for the clip that I had snapped to the chunky belt on my flowing skirt and twisted up my hair on the base of my neck, the slight wave of my dark brown, near-black hair annoying me today.

"Nothing's wrong. I'm just focusing."

"Well, that's a lie, but I'll let you keep it. Because I know Sage and Laurel won't let you lie for long."

I narrowed my eyes at the other woman. "You're getting spooky, missy."

"So says the witch." She winked as two more tourists walked in, both mundanes unable to see the magic around them. But they didn't snicker or sneer. Instead, they looked curious, and as I let my wind magic settle around me, focusing on the curiosity escaping them, I nodded in approval before letting Esmeralda do what she did best.

Many mundanes and others came into our shop wanting to see a witch. While I might look like one, with my flowing skirts and blunt bangs, or even when I went full-on CEO in my dark suit pants and business tops, I wasn't what most were looking for. Esmeralda was the perfect late- to mid-'90s era witch from one of our favorite movies. She had the piercings, the black spiky hair, chunky boots, and a short, black dress that moved around her hips as she swayed. She looked like a natural witch, and tourists loved it. I looked like either a businesswoman or a fortune teller, depending on my day. Today, I was more of a cross between the two and couldn't be bothered to really care. I hadn't slept the night before; dreams of lives past slamming into me with each passing moment.

I knew why, of course. *Ash.* As soon as Ash had stepped foot into Ravenwood to protect his sister, the memories of who we had once been had come forth. I could still remember the day that we had given ourselves to one another fully. Not just our bodies, as we had done that before, but in a way that had been pure magic, a blending of who we could be and what connected the two of us.

Because of that, I had lost him.

My chest ached again, and I did my best to ignore it because I was truly afraid of what would happen next. Not that I would allow fear to be the one thing that came at me. I needed to be stronger than this. I needed to not let fear drive every ounce of who I was.

Anyway, I couldn't not think about Ash. Not when he haunted my dreams, and he was always there. No matter what I did, he was there. Although he only stepped foot into my shop in order to be with the coven and the rest of our circle, I still felt as if he were always there.

I did not want to think about Ash, so I wasn't going to. Instead, I went to work on my shop, the herbs, everything that I needed to be as a full businesswoman. I had opened the shop after Ash had left. After I had been left behind by not only by him but by the others. After all, somebody had needed to stay in Ravenwood to keep its wards secure, and my aunt hadn't been able to do it on her own. When she died, I had been the only one left. The final Ravenwood.

It didn't seem possible in a town that was named after my family, but everyone else was gone. There were no more connections. And with the way that my life was going, I would be the last Ravenwood. No more generations would come after me.

The one person that was supposed to be mine, my soulmate, was gone. Oh, the husk of who he might have once been still roamed the town, but Ash wasn't mine. I couldn't have a soulmate, couldn't have a future with a man with no soul.

With that, I told myself it was the final time I would think about Ash.

I went back to work, spoke with a few more tourists, and Frank, the old jaguar shifter who hobbled in. He had been injured in an attack a few months ago, and I knew he was still in pain but was doing better. He smiled up at me as I came down the spiral staircase from my office, and I went towards him and hugged him tightly.

"You're looking mighty fit, Frank."

He wiggled his brows, then kissed me on the cheek. "Only for you, Rowen."

"Well, I appreciate it. Is there something I can do for you?"

"I was stopping in to see your face before I head over to Sage's bakery. I'm craving some honey twists."

His eyes danced with laughter, and I grinned. I couldn't help it. He was a cranky old jaguar who might not be able to race as fast as he once could, but he was a sweet older man who I adored. I didn't know what I would've done if we had lost him in that attack.

"You better be careful. I saw a few bear cubs out there earlier. You may run out of honey twists."

He guffawed. "Sage always leaves one for me. She knows to hide them from the big bears. Even with their sense of smell, they don't mess with the jaguar."

He wiggled his brows once more and I laughed, feeling far lighter as he walked away.

"He's such a nice man," Esmeralda said as we found ourselves in an empty shop. It was happening more often than not these days, the empty shop, the quiet times between rushes. Ravenwood was dying, and we all knew it. Yes, the town members could keep us afloat, with their outside jobs and us doing our best to keep them here. However, whatever was twisting our wards, leaving an oily slick that was taking more and more energy out of me with each passing day, seemed to be pushing the tourists away.

Honestly, even though I hated the idea that we may have to close some doors on Main Street one day soon if we weren't careful, I was grateful that some tourists weren't going to be here because they would be cannon fodder for the revenants. The walking dead that were controlled by the necromancers.

Necromancers were witches that turned to their dark side and twisted their magic, so they had a connection to the dead. They retained their elemental magic, but it was perverse and called to the souls and husks and bodies of those perished. They controlled those revenants and pushed them into the town, doing their best to kill everyone in their path. The strongest ones, most likely Oriel, could also control shades, actual spirits of those who were dead, rather than what was left behind when the spirit left.

Oriel and his team of witches and necromancers had desecrated grave upon grave to build up their army of revenants. They were using sites outside of Ravenwood itself, cemeteries we couldn't protect. Some news organizations had already picked up on the grave robbing. However, no one could put it together outside of small circles. Oriel was too smart for that, and while I wished he would make a mistake that would help us catch him, I didn't want him to make the mistake that would bring the eyes of the outside world to Ravenwood. We needed to protect its secrets, even if we weren't prepared for what would come if Oriel were any stronger than he was.

The bell over the door jingled again, and I smiled wide as Sage and Laurel walked in.

Laurel's now vibrant red hair was a mass of curls around her face as if she hadn't bothered to blow it out that morning. She was gorgeous and filled with so much life that I nearly envied her. But I could only be grateful because we had almost lost her. The Christopher curse that had taken her brother from me had nearly taken her from me as well. Had nearly taken her mate from us, too. She winked at me, the fire dancing in her eyes, nothing to do with an abundance of power that she couldn't control, but everything to do with the happiness in her gaze. Yes, we were on the brink of another battle, war heading towards us far too quickly for either one of our own goods, but Laurel was happy.

Just as happy as the woman with the chestnut hair beside her. Sage was a newer witch, one who hadn't known of her powers until she stepped foot into Ravenwood. A spell, most likely done by Oriel himself, had kept Sage away from us for far longer than we had ever known. It wasn't until that spell had been broken, purposely, that Sage had made her way here, shattered and in need of family. She had found that family in us.

But now she was here, her water element strong, and getting stronger day by day. We three were the coven, keeping the town safe, and we were strong enough to take out Oriel.

No matter what my dreams might think.

"I didn't know you were coming in this early, since you both have work," I said as I hugged them both close. I moved away so Esmeralda could do the same, and then my staffer pushed me out of the door. "Go, enjoy the rest of your day with your friends. I can handle this."

"I thought I was the boss," I teased.

"You are, now go train, get stronger, I can deal with the bits and bobs that come with tourists."

She winked as she said it, and I shook my head, clasped hands with both Sage and Laurel, and headed out. "You know, that sounds like a plan."

"You have bags under your eyes and deep, dark shadows," Laurel whispered. "Why aren't you sleeping?"

I raised my chin, annoyed Laurel could see me so easily. "I do love the fact that, even through a glamour, you're always good at making sure I know exactly what I look like. Thank you for reminding me I look like crap."

"That's not what she meant," Sage added, then winced. "Okay, maybe that's what she meant. You do look tired, Rowen. Did you not sleep?"

"I'm fine." My magic pushed at me, disagreeing.

"You're fine because you couldn't sleep because of something else, or because the wards are continuing to hurt you?"

I scowled at her. "What's with this bluntness?"

"I'm always blunt. You're usually better at sidestepping. That worries me more than anything."

But, before I could say anything, there was a scream

over the bridge, and we turned as one, our magic rising towards the surface.

"Revenants," Sage whispered, and I nodded, watching the twisted way the mist came forward. It was a dark fog, shadows, that spoke of the magic of Oriel and his team.

We'd had a reprieve for the past month, while Oriel must have been regaining his power. After all, we had killed many of his team members, and his second-in-command had been hurt, nearly killed, by Laurel during the final battle of fire and flame.

But it seemed he was back, and as the first revenant came forward, its body at a harsh angle as if its back has been broken, its skin sliding off its bones, I pulled forth on the magic and prayed we would be strong enough.

Only as the second, and the third, and the next dozen came forward, I had a feeling we wouldn't be enough at all.

CHAPTER
THREE

Ash

My feet pounded along the pavement as I ran towards the mist that hid the revenants. I cursed under my breath as I tried to move faster, the earth magic within me reaching out towards the disturbance.

A hawk cawed overhead, and I recognized Jaxton as he flew towards Laurel and the others.

Rome came out of the local lawyer's office, Ariel, his beta at his side. The bear alpha nodded tightly before he began running alongside me, Ariel with us.

"Revenants?" He growled the question.

I nodded. "Looks like. The girls have it, but they don't need to do it alone."

Rome gave me a look at that statement, and I held back a shrug. Because there wasn't any feeling in it. It was a statement. Clear. The coven, as it was in this incarnation, could handle things on their own. However, they did not need to. It was a waste of resources not to help them. It wasn't my empathy showing. I did not have any. I was a man without a soul.

The first revenant came towards Sage as the young witch had her arms out, water from the creek below slamming into the sides of the bridge. She was focusing on her power and doing much better than she had when I had first met her, but she was still learning.

With a flick of my wrist, I pulled at the rock bed below the water and slammed the stones into the revenant. Sage looked sharply over her shoulder at me before her eyes widened and she nodded before going back to fighting the hunk of bone and rotting flesh in front of her.

"Thank you," Rome whispered, and then he shifted. Bones and sinew twisted, forming into a large grizzly bear. Rome was huge, the biggest bear shifter I had ever seen. No, that wasn't quite right, now that I thought about it. Trace and Alden had been the same size after all. Triplets forever connected, even though two were now gone. It should hurt to think about Trace and Alden, the boys who had turned to men that I had grown up with. But there was nothing. There couldn't be anything.

That familiar voice screamed at me, though I could ignore it now. After all, I had long since silenced whatever tried to speak to me through the empty vastness that was my heart. The curse had done its job, and I was alone.

I shoved my magic into the earth again, watching the stones crumble behind the bridge.

"Are you trying to take down Ravenwood along the way?" Rowen snapped at me, her dark hair billowing in *her* wind. She was beautiful, stunning. I didn't need a soul to know that she was the most gorgeous creature out there. And the way that she used her magic only intensified that inherent beauty.

"I'm taking out the trash. Are you going to fault me for that?" My voice was cool, cultured, the same voice that got me into the top boardrooms and had made me my first million on my own by the time I was twenty. I didn't need morals in order to make my billions, though Laurel was the one that held me accountable. She was the one that made sure that the company wasn't like those that hurt others. Well, that small screaming part of me might've cared. The rest didn't. However, I was a Christopher, just like my sister, and I would do what she wanted in order to protect the family name.

I pushed thoughts of my day job out of my mind, as they didn't matter right now. Instead, I needed to focus on the magic in my veins and protecting the coven leader— the woman I had once loved. I couldn't love her anymore, but she was strength personified, even if she did her best to glamour away the dark circles under her eyes. She couldn't hide them from me, however. She never could, soul or not.

"We need the coven as a whole," Laurel panted, her flaming sword at her side. "There have to be dozens more, and we can't hide them from the tourists much longer."

I nodded tightly as I watched the three women come together, their magic pulsating.

"Ash, we need you," Laurel called.

Rowen's head whipped toward my sister. "We do not. We need the *coven*."

My sister scowled, her eyes aflame. "We need the power of the four elements. We don't have time to argue about it. Ash. Get over here."

"You need the four elements. You heard her. I'm earth. Just because you hate me doesn't mean you can ignore my magic." I gripped Laurel's hand tightly and Rowen scowled before she turned away, the lines of her face telling me I was going to hear about this later. Good, I would enjoy the fight. It was the one thing that sparked anything within me these days. Not even the magic pulling me in did much anymore.

The earth pulsated beneath my feet, reaching out towards me like it always did. It was hard to focus solely on the magic and not on everything else around me. It was as if whatever was lacking within me desperately craved something else to fill it. Only, there wasn't anything, and I needed to not allow my thoughts to go down that path.

"Repeat after me," Rowen called out above the shouts and revenants.

"Lord and Lady working for me and through me, heal this witch in her time of need. Bolster her strength, plant the seed. By air and water, earth and fire, banish the dark in these times most dire. Bring her peace, bathe her in light, make her whole this very night. With the power of the coven and blessings times three, this is my will, so mote it be."

Magic tore from me, the earth shaking beneath our feet as our four elements came together, a rarity when it came to spells with us, and the revenants were pushed back, the force of our magic far stronger than it had even been a week ago.

With the little witch, as well as Laurel's new powers as a phoenix, we were stronger. But only when Rowen deemed herself able to work beside me.

She quickly let go of my hand as if she'd been burned and I ignored her, as there was no feeling that came with it. Instead, I pressed my hands together, let the power float in me, and pushed out the magic, solidifying into a soil dagger. The dirt dug into the revenant in front of me, and I pushed again, beheading the monster. The revenant had once been human, had once had a soul, had feelings and hopes and dreams and fears. And yet, like me, they were now a husk of what they had once been. That they were rotted flesh over broken bone, and I was chiseled marble over ice. It wasn't lost on me that the differences were few and far between. I was one step away from a revenant, and yet I fought on the side of my family.

Of my coven.

Of Rowen.

And it was only the screaming part of me, the one that I could not hear fully, that kept me on this side at all.

I kept pushing against the other revenants as fae and shifters and the coven pushed and destroy the rest of the soulless. I couldn't sense the magic of the necromancer, so I didn't know if this was Renee—the lieutenant who had lost her mate and nearly been killed in the other battle—or Oriel himself. The bastard refused to fight with us head-on, and it was only through fighting with his lackeys that we even knew who this man was.

More revenants went down, one by one, and soon we were part of the cleanup.

Rowen walked away from me without another word, not even bothering to glance at me. I didn't even sigh. There was no point. This was what she wanted, me here to help but without being part of anything. And perhaps if I could focus on something beyond myself, I would know it was what I deserved. It was hard to know what that was when I could barely focus on anything other than trying to figure out what was on the path of good and what would turn me into what Oriel had become.

That was the problem with having no soul. I was one bad spell, one poor decision, away from becoming Oriel himself. And if I was able to fear, that's what I would worry about.

"Rome and the others are dealing with any of the public that may have seen something they shouldn't have. Do you want to help me fix this bridge?" Jaxton asked as the hawk shifter shoved himself into pants. I sighed and looked over at the man who had once been my friend. I wasn't sure if I could call him that now, not when I had ice in my veins and I couldn't feel anything unless I told myself to.

"What do you need?"

"You have any magic left within you to help secure the base? I know your magic wasn't what pushed away part of the building blocks here, but between erosion, revenants, and spell after spell, it could use some resurfacing."

I nodded and rolled up my shirtsleeves. My anchors around my wrist shifted slightly, the trees billowing in their own wind. At one point, I thought that the wind had been Rowen. That our anchors had come together, her breeze through the trees, that sent vibration to my own earth magic. Only, without a bond between us, I knew that wasn't the case. We were separate entities, never to twine again.

"What else do you need from me?" I asked.

Jaxton met my gaze. "Anything you have to give, Ash. That's always been the case."

I held back a frown at that, wondering where he was going with those thoughts of his, but then went to work.

This was something I could do. Cleaning up messes, perhaps of my own making, and then once the foundations of the bridge were back in place and the stones felt secure, I went to help fix part of the cement barrier that some might think were for floods but were to help direct some of the water magic from Sage. When waves crested over the bridge it made a mess, and so we did our best to try to funnel the water in certain places so we could use it against the revenants.

The fact that our town was slowly becoming a battleground, complete with infrastructure changes to allow that to happen, should worry me, and yet it just felt rote at this point.

The others were still speaking, discussing points of the battle or future plans. No one came to me. I had once been best friends with Rome, Jaxton, Trace, and Alden. And now there was nothing. Rowen had walked away while Rome held Sage's hand, and my sister leaned into her mate. The four of them were a unit, their own circle within the coven circle itself, and I had nothing.

I held back a sigh and made my way back to my home.

The Christopher home had long since burned to the ground, our curses fire for anything that came near. Laurel lived in an older home that she had redone over time. Sometimes she stayed there with Jaxton. Sometimes they stayed with the wing, above the ground in the aerie with the other hawks.

I had bought a McMansion of sorts on the end of

Main Street. The opposite end from Rowen's family home. I hadn't done that on purpose, or perhaps maybe part of me had. The place was far too large for me, and it echoed when I spoke, but it seemed good enough. I had worked long and hard to be where I was. It was nice to see the fruits of my labor.

I was just turning down the path when a small yip hit my ears. I froze, wondering what that sound could be. A whine echoed throughout the trees, and I ran towards it.

The growl hit me first, the slobbering mess of the revenant crawling towards the wolf pup hidden below a fallen branch.

From what I could tell, the revenant had escaped from the others and had trapped this tiny wolf pup with the tree itself. I cursed and spoke under my breath.

"Earth, air, water, fire, bring us that which we desire. Stop this evil, purge this blight, banish this death to darkest night. Lord and Lady, ancestors, too, lend us your strength for what we must do. Take this darkness so we may be free. This is our will, so mote it be!"

I didn't have the strength of coven or that magic, but this spell created a bubble around the wolf pup and then I took a branch, slashed out, and beheaded the revenant.

The wolf pup yipped at me, let out a tiny little bark, but when the spell dissipated, the little pup ran towards me on four legs and jumped into my arms. It shifted back into a naked toddler, and I held them close, wondering where the hell their parents were.

"Hello, child," I said, my voice wooden.

"Thank you," the baby cried as he stuck his head underneath my chin and wept.

"Lucas! Lucas!" A woman shouted as she ran towards me.

I hadn't known that more wolves had moved into the area, as we were a predominantly bear town, and when she saw me holding her child, she must've gotten the wrong impression. I didn't blame her after all.

Fangs erupted from her gums, her claws came out, and she narrowed her golden gaze. "Put down my son."

"If you would look to the left, you will see the dead revenant that I took care of. Your child seems unharmed, though the tree branch might have hurt him. I'm not sure, but from his whimpering, it seems to be from fear."

I held out the small child and the woman snatched him from me, her eyes wide.

"Mama. Ash saved me."

The woman's gaze immediately stopped glowing, her claws receding, and she held her small child close. "Thank you. I'm sorry."

I shook my head. "No worries. It would look startling to find a stranger holding your child in the forest."

"No, I shouldn't have thought the worst. You're Ash. One of the coven."

"I'm a witch, but my sister's of the coven." A small distinction that I wasn't sure if she understood. "Are you new to town then?"

She nodded tightly. "My friend moved here earlier with her triplet wolves. We needed a place to stay, one where we could have our freedom, and Rome has been quite welcoming."

I nodded tightly. "He is that. Keep an eye on your child. We are under war, and while it might be safer here than it would be in other places for shifters, it's still not a safe town."

"I understand." Her eyes full of knowing, before she looked behind me. "Rowen. Ash saved my son. Thank you for looking for him with me."

I had known Rowen was coming up from behind me. I always could tell. Her magic scraped against me, leaving a raw wound in its wake, that and the spicy scent of her always set me on edge, even though I didn't quite understand it anymore.

"I'm glad he's safe. Keep Lucas beside you at all times these days. We're trying to keep the town protected by its wards, but as you know, magic finds a way."

The woman nodded. "Thank you, Rowen." She looked at me. "Thank you, Ash. Seriously. Thank you. Lucas is my heart."

"Bye, Ash. Thank you, Ash." The toddler waved, and the woman and her son walked away, leaving me with a dead revenant at my feet and Rowen at my side.

"Why were you out alone?" Rowen snaped, and I sighed.

"Truly? That's what you're going to go with. I saved a small child, and yet I'm in trouble for being out alone."

"You left."

"As did you. Remember that, coven leader."

She scowled, the wind in the trees increasing. "Ash."

"Temper temper. I can feel your magic pulsating. It's waiting."

"And you're an asshole."

I snorted, but there wasn't any humor in it. "I never claimed not to be. You're the one that left to go deal with whatever you needed to. I was headed home to go to work. I saved a small child. How am I in the wrong here?" I asked.

"She thought you were coven."

"And why am I not?" I bit out.

She waved me off before glaring at me—a familiar look these days. "Why are you here, Ash? Why are you always making things so difficult?"

"I'm here to protect this town. And my sister. I might not have a soul anymore, but I have responsibilities. It's time you understood that." I paused as she opened her mouth, probably to yell at me again. "And it's time we did something about it. I came to your house before to tell you, and you've ignored me. We don't have any more time."

She threw her hands in the air, far more emotion from her than I usually saw. She was so good at pretending to be cool and collected—the knowledgeable witch, but she wasn't always. "It will kill you."

"And how is that any worse than what we're already dealing with? That's the thing, Rowen. Maybe I've been dead a lot longer than you think. Who knows. But something is screaming. Something needs to change. We're the ones that are supposed to work together."

She pressed her lips into a thin line. "You don't know that."

"We both know that. And it's time you realize it. I can be of assistance."

"You walked away from that responsibility a long time ago. Don't pretend that you suddenly care."

"Don't pretend that you stopped caring at all."

And with that, I walked away, once again not knowing how to speak to Rowen. It was time that we changed things. Time that we set the record straight.

It was time to perhaps find a way to get my soul back.

And that meant that it was time for me to die.

CHAPTER

FOUR

Rowen

I knew I could get angry, but I hadn't realized that he could make me so angry so quickly. It burned within me like the fire magic that seared Laurel's veins. I stood in my garden, letting the cool air brush my face, trying to cool down the heat blazing my cheeks.

Everything ached. My heart, head, and my soul. My connection to Ravenwood itself.

I had spent my entire life, it seemed, trying to keep Ravenwood alive, to keep it safe, and even with the coven now, I was failing.

I knew I couldn't allow the others to think about that, couldn't think about the history that lay behind my name and exactly who I was. Instead, I focused on the fact that I was so angry at Ash.

He had put himself in jeopardy walking around the woods alone, and I couldn't be angry at him for it because he had saved Lucas. The small wolf pup and his mother had just recently moved to town because Ravenwood was supposed to be a safe space for shifters, fae, and magic alike, and yet, I was not strong enough to protect them all.

The coven was supposed to be the ones that protected them, who rose together to keep the world safe and the secrecy of who we were. And yet, something was twisting that. Somebody was going through the weave of our magic and untangling it strand by strand, as if they knew exactly how our ancestral spells worked.

The Princes, the Christophers, and the Ravenwoods were the three founding families of this town. Together the three of them had woven an intricate blanket of wards to guard those who needed that protection. And yet, it seemed as if somebody knew and understood the intricacies of how the spells themselves operated. And they knew exactly how to touch one thread for it to unravel. I was spending far too much of my energy to piece it back together, to sew in the piecework that wasn't a full weave. I wasn't quilting. I was in triage.

And the others didn't know it. They knew something was wrong, but I couldn't rely on them. Not that I didn't trust them. They were my heart and my soul and everything that I could ever want. They were my family. But

Sage wasn't strong enough yet. Oh, she was thousands of times stronger than she had been when she had first fallen into the town of Ravenwood and saved her mate's life. She was growing into her magic leaps and bounds and was becoming who she needed to be, and with each passing day, she was giving me and this town more of her strength. But we couldn't take it all. She couldn't siphon enough. She would open up her heart and let everything go, and she would become the husk of who she once was, like a shade a necromancer could wield.

Laurel was only now thriving after an entire life of dying because of her magic. The Christopher curse had caused her to die slowly day by day, acid drip by acid drip, as she used her magic. I couldn't ask her before to use her magic to protect the town. Just breathing had been killing her, using magic to keep the core of what Ravenwood was safe? No, that would have been suicide.

So, I alone had been the one to protect the core of magic. No one else could do it. Not the shifters, not the fae. I knew that my great-grandparents had even tried that, and it had failed spectacularly. They had tried to use the combined forces of what coven they had. Even though it had been more than three, they had still been weaker than us because of the magic they possessed. That magic hadn't been enough, even combined with that of the hawk shifters and bear shifters. Even the former wolf pack that had once lived here before they had moved on to another town had tried to help. And it hadn't been enough. The wolf pack had moved on because of their own politics and hierarchy issues, and those seem to be coming to a head once again, as parts of their packs were now moving back to Ravenwood.

How was I to provide a safe harbor when it wasn't safe at all? A child almost died today, and I hadn't been there.

A revenant had broken through the ranks, had slipped through the trees as if he were part of the mist itself, and had nearly killed Lucas. Only Ash's quick thinking on a chance of walking back home alone when he had, had protected that child. Would I have been able to catch that revenant if I had stayed with the others? That question would haunt me until the end of my days because I knew I had left, not because the work was done. No, I had left because of Ash. I left because looking at him hurt. And I never let anybody in on that. Oh, they all guessed, and they talked behind my backs, and I let them. It was what friends did. They worried, and they tried to find answers when there were none.

They all knew my deepest pains, and I couldn't let them in on any more secrets. I couldn't let them know that when I saw Ash, I saw a betrayal of the deepest kind. A jagged edge of a knife digging into my heart as it cored out pieces of me.

My Ash was gone, and this cold marble statue of a man that had come back to town was not the man I had loved.

When the bond had broken between us, I had felt like

I died. Now, I stared into the eyes of a man who no longer recognized me as his, or even as anybody who could be on his side. I wanted to blame him for that. I wanted to blame him for everything. But I couldn't because it was the Christopher curse. While Laurel had broken hers, the act of the curse itself disallowed Ash to even fight against what was killing him slowly, inch by inch.

I understood the ramifications of the powers beyond us, I did, and yet all I could do was rage at the gods and a fate for giving me a mate who could not be mine. A soulmate with no soul was not a mate. You didn't just take off part of a word and suddenly make its own entity. He was not mine, and yet he had almost died today. He could be alone. And I was so angry that I cared. That I couldn't just walk away and not have my past mistakes and heartache be thrown at my face every time I tried to take a breath. I stood on my ancestral grounds, in a garden I spent hours and hours each day trying to grow and nurture and breathe life into, and I cried.

I let the tears fall, tears I never let anyone else see. They needed to see a strong coven leader, one who let her emotions out but didn't let herself break down in front of others. They needed a shoulder to lean on; I could not bow down before them and break.

So now I stood, looking at the two-story structure from colonial times. I had painted recently, dark black with blues to make it look like the perfect witch's home you would see online, and people would say, "Yes, that's where they wanted to live." But they wouldn't understand that this was my home. My grandmother's grandmother's grandmother had lived here. The Ravenwood's had built this place, had thought of the turrets and the wraparound porch and the attic with our spells and pentagrams. They had thought of everything that they could possibly do in their time to build a future for those who needed protection.

But over time, ultimate power corrupts. Or perhaps it faded away. There had not been one instance I could mark in the histories that I read of the Ravenwood's that told me when we had begun to fail. The Christophers had been cursed, and that was a large instance, as children's children began to perish, and magic hadn't come in fruition until too late, or not at all.

The Princes had been driven out of town, with only Penelope staying after so many years. But then Penelope had died, at the hands of Oriel's right hand, Faith. She had died, but not before taking too many of our people with her.

I let out a breath, thinking of all that who had perished. There was still Prince blood out in the world, same as Christopher's. Though they were second cousins, or three-times-removed aunts and uncles. But they existed. And though they might not practice magic, within their souls was a hope. And that hope brought forth the magic of the coven. That was how ancestral magic worked.

And if we survived this darkness that had been fore-told by my ancestors, the founders of Ravenwood itself, there would be more generations.

Sage and Rome would bring forth powerful children, even if they weren't pure witches or shifters. Just the love that they were brought into would be power enough. The same with the hawks and witches when Laurel and Jaxton brought forth children.

While I would never tell them to have children for the sake of the coven, I knew both couples deeply desired children and wanted a future. Laurel hadn't thought she would survive to give birth, let alone want to bring a child into the Christopher curse, but she had broken that part of her line and couldn't send it forth. Any Christopher child that was born of Jaxton and Laurel's union would not be cursed. They would have their own future to thrive in.

Ash was the final person with his curse. Would his death break it? I shuddered at the cold thought and slid my hand through the hibiscus flowers, letting my fingers dance along the petals. I inhaled their sweet scent, then looked over the ivy running up the trellis near the turret on my home. I needed to work in the garden more, but I couldn't focus. I could only hear the screaming of those who had nearly been hurt by the revenants. Somehow we were all unharmed. The revenants that had come towards us from Oriel or Renee, or someone else we didn't know who was working with Oriel himself, hadn't been strong this time. They had been at the end of their line, their presence weak. And I only had to wonder if it was all a distraction. That's something else might be coming for us.

I went to the ground, dug my fingers into the soil, and called on my magic.

"Lord and lady, hear my plea. Send forth light and growth in harmony.

Earth, wind, water, fire, we are the ones the magic desires.

Bring forth hope and growth and future.

So you will, so mote it be."

Magic hummed through me, and I smiled, letting the earth know that I was here, and I was as whole as I could be.

I once again wiped away another tear, but this time added it to my soil. The tears of the lost could be magic in itself. I was losing everything. I had lost everything.

Every time I worked in my garden, I thought of him. Of the Ash who would help me plant so many of these, would help me weed out what had been barren or damaged over time. He had helped this place thrive; it had been ours and not just mine. For he was of earth, and I was of air. We had been missing our water, but Sage was now so strong and could do anything. I knew it.

But Ash was not here to help, and therefore this was all mine.

There was a sound of a branch breaking, and I whirled, my hands outstretch, ready to fight. The first revenant came, my magic screamed, calling out to my coven, hoping they would hear. It was a new spell we were working on that connected us through the bonds that made us coven. We three women who then could tell our soulmates, or in essence, Laurel and Sage could tell their soulmates who they were bonded to, that there was a warning. And we would go where we needed to, to protect the town as a whole rather than this one spot we were fighting.

Only, no one would be able to tell Ash.

I quickly jammed that from my mind, telling myself it wasn't productive. Yearning over a man who was never mine would only lead to my death. And as the first revenant came out, this one far newer and stronger than the ones earlier, I picked up the shovel next to me. I didn't want to use up the entirety of my magic, use spell after spell that would just take time to try to fight these. I needed time and space in order to create a spell. Therefore, I would use whatever weapon in my arsenal, including the air magic that I could push into small tornadoes or breezes, in order to get at whoever was coming at me.

The first revenant came at me, its fingers curled into claws as it rushed. I sent air down my shovel as I slammed into it, knocking it three feet back as it rolled onto its feet. It was fast, diligent, and I cursed under my breath.

Another revenant came at me, this one wearing a tailored suit, as if they had been buried in it and recently been uncovered. Bile rose in my throat, and I pushed away all thoughts of who this man had been, his family, or whatever he had gone through in his life. He looked like a young man, early twenties, with his whole life ahead of him, and now he was dead, his body desecrated thanks to a necromancer.

No matter how much power dark magic may bring to another, I had never once thought about going down that path. I knew who I was and what the coven needed of me. I would never become that darkness itself, even for the extra power to keep me alive.

Becoming a dark witch turns you toward necromancy and you lose your soul, but not in the way that Ash had. His had been ripped from him in a screaming embrace while a necromancer still had the dark and tainted rotted soul of one who would enter our version of hells in a fiery cascade.

I fisted my left hand, then let it open quickly, a burst of air pushing through, and slamming into the man. He fell back, staggering, but came forward quickly, and I cursed again, this time holding my palm out, lifting him into the air, and then back down in a cutting motion, sending a wave of air towards the other man. He fell back into another revenant, but they kept coming, another dozen sliding out of the trees, all of them so strong. *So strong.* I could barely breathe. I pushed out my magic towards the coven, hoping they would hear my pleas. That I was alone. My inner wards of my home being broken down bit by bit, and I didn't understand how. How was Oriel getting through so quickly? The only ones that could break through my ward so quickly were those who knew of my magic, and it didn't make any sense. How could this necromancer abide so much magic at once?

I slammed out with my shovel, decapitating one revenant, and then shoved it into the chest of another. I shot out both hands, the shovel being ripped from my grip. A shocking blast of air hit two more revenants, but they kept coming. One gripped my arm, its claws digging into me, and I screamed, blood pooling. I slammed my feet into the ground, a tunnel of air pushing in between us. I nearly fell back, knowing it had been the only way to keep him off me. And then another revenant came, and another, and I was overrun. They were surrounding me, but except for that one that had grabbed me, that had hurt me, they weren't doing anything but corralling me. It didn't make any sense. I'd never seen revenants react with such control like this. What did they want?

Fear coated my tongue as I turned in circles, my air ready to push at any moment, but something else was coming. I could feel it along my spine, dripping closer, and I sucked in a breath as a man in a dark suit came forward. His dark hair fell over his brow, his eyes black with a slight red rim, as if he had been using so much dark magic over his lifeline, he was the one rotting from the inside out rather than the revenants.

I told myself not to scream, not to react, but how was I supposed to do anything else but shout for help? Because

I knew who this was. This man in a dark suit, a slight beard over his strong jaw, and a wicked grin that told me he used it for lecherous things.

I tried to maintain my balance as I looked at the man that I knew to be Oriel.

The dark necromancer.

He smiled softly and it made my skin crawl. "Well done. For a woman by yourself, you sure do know how to fight."

"Bastard. You let other people die for you when you're suddenly here? We must've killed all your other help."

His jaw ticked, and I knew I had hit a sore spot. Good. Because if I could keep him talking, maybe the others would get here in time. I was strong, damn strong, and if I use the combined power of my own magic reserves, maybe I could take him out. Only I felt the power within the revenants surrounding me, caging me, as well as the magic Oriel himself, and I was deeply afraid I wasn't going to be enough.

"You will pay for Faith and perhaps the hawk. But Renee lives. My lieutenant. You tried your best with her, with that fire bitch, but Renee is alive. And she will have her revenge against the hawk and his phoenix whore."

I had to keep him talking. "You keep speaking, and yet I hear nothing. What power do you think you have to come to my town, to my rightful birthplace, and think you can overtake us? We are Ravenwood. We are stronger than you. No matter the magic that you call forth, you will never be us."

Oriel threw his head back and laughed, the air around us shaking.

And then I knew what kind of magic that this sorcerer had.

I knew who he could be.

He had air, like me. And he was strong. Far stronger than he should be in air, considering his dark magic brought forth the necromancy, not the air itself.

"Oh, darling, you're so naive."

"Who are you?" I asked, a stunning realization slowly sliding over me as I tried to catch my breath. Instead, the man just smiled and pulled up his shirtsleeves slightly. The pentagram on his forearm mirrored the one on Ash's, and I swallowed hard, looking at the runes etched on his arms that I knew went up to his torso. He probably glamoured them when he was out in public, but I knew what those were. Necromancer runes that took him to the side of darkness, that gave him his power.

But it was that jawline, the cheekbones, those eyes. Because they were not of the darkness; I knew those eyes.

Those were my father's eyes.

"Who are you?" I asked again, my voice a rasp.

"Oh, darling. It's taking you long enough. Daddy dearest never told you about me?"

"Liar," I spat, my world crumbling around me as his words took root.

"It's okay. It's really okay. Your dad was a bastard, and again, so am I, isn't that right? He had me long before he even met your dearest mother. But he never came back for me. So, you see, you're not the last of the Ravenwoods, dear sister of mine. I'm older. I am the rightful heir to the Ravenwood power. I should be the head of the coven and the holder of the core of this town. And because you can't seem to be the one to hold it yourself, I'll have to do what was my right all along. Take it for myself."

"You're delusional if you think that that's true. Nothing of what you said is true."

"Look into your heart, dearest sister. Sense my magic. You know that we're related. And you're not the last of the Ravenwoods. That everything that you thought was a lie. But what could you possibly have ever wanted? You're nothing. And you're going to die here one day, just like you always thought you would. Alone, bleeding out, and wondering if this was the one moment you could have changed everything. That you could have come to my side and ruled with me as my sister, the Ravenwoods of the town, who hold the power to control the magic of this world."

I couldn't believe what he was saying. He had to be lying. He *was* a liar. Only, I was truly afraid he wasn't this time. "Fuck. You."

Oriel smirked, even as I tried to come to terms with exactly what he was saying. It didn't make any sense. It couldn't. This wasn't true. And yet, it felt like it was true, and I was going to throw up.

This was my brother? My father's son. He must not have known. He couldn't have known. And yet I knew those eyes. I knew that magic. I could taste it.

This was why he could get into the town so easily, why he could twist the weave of the wards, and why he could be on my property at all.

Because he was our blood.

I had keyed the wards and the safety of this town to my blood because I was the final Ravenwood.

And my mistake was going to cost us all.

"You're so sweet, but you're going to die soon. Not today. I'm not done with you yet. But soon."

I shoved up all of my magic, as much as I could, calling forth the power of Ravenwood itself, digging into the core, something I rarely did because it would hurt and it would take part of me in doing so, and I pushed out my air magic, slicing each of the revenants in half. Oriel threw his head back and laughed once more before shifting into a dark wolf with black and red eyes.

The wolf that Sage had seen when she had first come to town.

It was real.

I screamed as the wolf leaped, digging its fangs into my shoulder, and as it tore at my flesh, I shoved my air magic into it, pushing at Oriel, and he leaped away, running into the mist and into the forest, and I fell, my legs collapsing.

My breath came in pants as I felt the warm blood seep into my clothes, and I lay on top of the corpses of the revenants that were no longer moving.

As the warmth of my blood, my life, seeped into the ground, I called on my coven once more.

But, once again, they never came.

CHAPTER
FIVE

Ash

Something tugged on the inner core of my chest, and I rubbed over the burn, wondering what the hell that could be. I frowned, my feet moving before I even realized I was running. I slammed out of the front door, nearly jumping off the covered patio, and ran through the forest behind the homes and businesses on Main Street. I didn't want to deal with questioning looks or have someone stop me to ask where I was going. Others feared me because they knew what I had lost and were afraid I was one step away from becoming Oriel. I couldn't focus on their desires or what they wanted. Or who they thought I could be. I could only focus on the pain ripping from me. It was as if an unknown source was pulling at the bond itself, yet I *had* no bond. It had broken long ago, but the echo of what it once had been screamed in agony, and I ran.

I pushed harder, calling out my magic. The tendrils of who I was as a witch and what magic I could hold as a man dove into the earth itself, spreading out in a fan to find out where I was going, and yet I knew. I knew what called to me.

Who called to me.

I broke through the tree line and nearly sagged as I saw her there. Bodies laid in pieces, in piles, and yet it was her dark hair that I saw first, the blood covering her neck, her shoulders, her arms, the fact that she lay across a dead revenant.

I cursed under my breath and ran, falling to her side as I gently plucked her up off the corpse and held her close. Her eyes fluttered open, and her mouth parted, that grayness in her gaze filled with shock, fear, and uncertainty. Her skin was clammy to the touch, and I ran my hands down her body to check for broken bones. I nearly sagged in relief at the knowledge there were only a few cuts on bruises along the outside, but I had no idea what had happened to her internally.

How could I read her so easily after so many years away? It was as if these were memories of a distant past, and yet I knew this was the present, and she was hurt.

"Ash," she whispered, blood on her lips.

I cursed under my breath and picked her up, aware that she was covered in blood not her own. And yet, there was too much that was hers as well.

"I've got you," I whispered, even as the numbness settled over my chest, that echo of a bond no longer in evidence.

"The coven. They didn't come."

I frowned at that thought, feeling as if something was wrong with the statement. Laurel and Sage would never leave Rowen unsafe and unprotected unless something held them back. "What happened?"

"Why didn't they come?"

I set Rowen down on the kitchen island, knowing she would have hated if I got blood on her couch. She was probably going to be upset that I set her here anyway. I didn't care.

"Rowen. Talk to me. What happened?" I cupped her face in my hands, meeting her gaze. She blinked as if coming out of a daze and swallowed hard.

"It was Oriel. He was here."

Ice settled over my skin, and I let the cool rage burn over me.

"He was here. He did this to you?"

"He sent the revenants." She swallowed hard as I pulled out the first aid kit. Her kit was unique to her and most witches' homes, as it contained herbs and poultices mixed with bandages and other Western medicine.

I did my best not to let my anger take control. I might

not be able to make choices that were right or wrong, but I could still hate. Still want to rip someone's head of for daring to touch her. "I saw the revenants. You did all of that? Taking them out, I mean."

She winced, her fingers playing along the edge of the bite mark. *A fucking bite mark.*

"I pulled on the core of the town, Ash."

I cursed under my breath, taking a moment to figure out what meds she needed. "Did it hurt? Are you okay? Fuck, Rowen, you know you're not supposed to do that. We don't know the ramifications or consequences on using magic we don't understand and is far greater than the coven itself."

I said the words, and yet I couldn't force myself to care more than I already did. There was nothing within me, just anger and silence, and yet I couldn't hate it. Because nothing within me was allowed to do that.

"I had to. It was the only way without the coven."

"And Oriel was here? I take it he is the bite mark. Did he shift into a wolf then?" I asked wryly.

Her eyes widened. "How did you know?" The uncertainty and fear in her tone should have sliced through me, but it didn't. It couldn't.

"We always thought that if Oriel was a true necromancer, with the power that he had, he could shift."

She narrowed her eyes at me. "We thought it was a possibility, not an inevitability. Yet, here we are, he is that wolf. The wolf that Sage saw."

I nodded tightly, cleaning the wound. "Good news, you can't be turned into a shifter."

"I don't appreciate your tone," she bit out crisply.

"I don't appreciate being forced to come here by a bond that doesn't exist."

She froze, and I could have rightly smacked myself for even mentioning it. "You felt me. That's why you're here?"

I sighed and bandaged up the wound after adding part of her spell. "Yes. Something tugged at me. Apparently, staying within the town for as long as I have has allowed magic to seep its way into my pores. Far more than usual. I don't know if I appreciate it."

She looked at me then and pressed her lips together.

"Say it. Just say it."

"What do you want me to say? Thank you? For saving my life, I suppose. As you can see, I did fine on my own. Oriel is gone for now. And I need to talk to the coven."

I couldn't help the sneer on my face. "And not me? How nice. And you should say thank you. I am cleaning your wounds, after all."

"And leaving a bloody mess in my kitchen. You know I have a workshop for this."

I frowned. "I don't, actually. Did you add that after I moved away?" She looked as if I had slapped her, and I held back another sigh. "I apologize."

She shook her head and held up her hand, her face holding a little more color than it had before. Of course, since she'd looked like a damn corpse along with the revenants, that wasn't saying much. "No, I'm in pain, and I'm grouchy. I could really use a drink."

"That I can do. Wine or whiskey?"

She stared at me for a moment before looking away, the pain at the edge of her eyes grating on me more than I cared to admit. "Get the whiskey. I could use the edge even if I don't like it."

"Is it in the same place?"

She nodded tightly, and I went to the liquor cabinet and poured each of us two fingers of the amber liquid. I handed her the glass, clinked mine to hers, and swallowed it all in one gulp. A fiery burn slid down my throat, and I set the crystal glass on the counter next to her and shook my head.

"Any more wounds I need to worry about?"

"You healed the ones on my neck and arms. I should be fine. I'll let the coven help me heal fully later."

"Again, not me." My jaw clenched.

"You're not part of the coven. You know that, Ash."

"I do. I always have." That had always been a problem, not that we'd ever discussed it.

The door slammed open at that moment and my sister stood there, her fiery red hair billowing around her as if she had pulled in the wind herself, even though that wasn't her element. I was surprised I didn't see a scorched trail of fire behind her.

"We saw the revenants. Why didn't you call us?" Laurel stated as she walked in, Sage right on her tail.

The little witch shook her head at my sister. "Laurel. Don't snap at her. Oh my god. You're hurt." Both women moved to Rowen's side, gripping her hands, and I edged out of the way, knowing I wasn't wanted anymore.

"What happened?" Rome asked, his gaze steely as he looked over the women before looking back to me.

"She'll have to tell you herself. Interesting, though, that none of you felt her call out to you until just now. Fascinating."

"I'd say it's interesting that you're here when I know for a fact you were at home until recently. Considering we just spoke," Jaxton drawled, and I shrugged.

"Again. Talk to her."

"I see we're drinking," Laurel said after a moment, looking between us, before she nodded tightly and pulled out four more glasses. "Am I going to need a drink for this?"

Rowen ran her hands through her dark hair. "Yes. I think I need more."

"Not with those wounds you don't. You're not going to heal completely if you're drunk," I growled, unaware I was even saying the words until I'd already done so.

What the hell was wrong with me? I hadn't reacted like this in years, and yet here I was, lashing out when I shouldn't even care.

"I know what to do with my own body, thank you very much," Rowen snapped.

"I don't want to get in the middle of this, but I agree

with Ash here, though not with all the growling," Sage added and winced. "I'm sorry. You're healing. You're obviously hurt, though Ash seemed to have done a good job of taking care of your wounds. Why don't we get you on the couch, covered in a blanket, with some hot tea?"

"And maybe we'll add whiskey to the tea if you're good," Laurel added as Sage rolled her eyes.

"Fine. Fine." Sage let out a small growl of her own that had my lips twitching before we all settled into the living room.

Finally situated, Rowen let out a breath. "You didn't hear me when I called for you?"

"We didn't know anything was wrong until just now," Laurel answered. "Why don't you start from the beginning."

I leaned against the wall across from the others, slightly apart. Rowen's home was different than it had been when we were younger. Though I had been in the place since I had returned, specifically that night when we had discussed my soul and what needed to be done, I still hadn't truly taken it in.

There were antiques around, and much of the layout and moldings and fireplaces were from the original home, or at least an update from a hundred years ago, but Rowen had added her own touch. Plants were everywhere, as were little touches of copper pots and black and gray decorations. It looked like her, or at least the her I had once known. She had always tried to be a gardener, had put a lot of herself into that part of her home. However, it had been something we used to do together, because of my affinity for earth while she had only had air. Not that there was anything *only* about her.

I had loved this home from the moment I had stepped foot in it. At one point, I had been jealous that the Raven-wood family home still stood while the Christopher home had been burned down before I was born. However, I couldn't be jealous of a place that Rowen had thrived in.

And now, I truly couldn't be jealous because it was hard to do so without caring. And my lack of soul prevented that—something I had to repeatedly tell myself these days.

"I was standing in the garden, working on weeding and other things, when the revenants came."

"How many?" Jaxton asked.

"At least a dozen. Their bodies are still out there." Rowen let out a breath, and Sage moved forward, gently taking Rowen's hand.

"What else happened?" Rome asked, his voice deep. He took up a sentinel position behind Sage and I almost envied the easy way the little witch leaned into him as if she trusted him with every part of her. Had Rowen ever been like that? I wasn't sure. She'd always been independent, a strength and pillar because of her duty and name. I had always been on the outside, even if I hadn't realized it until I'd walked away.

"They were stronger than the revenants we had fought

earlier. So strong, in fact, that even with a shovel and my air magic, I was afraid I wasn't going to be enough. I called to you, though it seems that you couldn't hear me. They were organized and skilled. Organized to the point that they surrounded me and didn't move on me. Instead, they waited for Oriel to show."

Alarms prickling, I moved forward, unsure of what I was hearing. "What?"

"You heard me. They stood around me, waiting for him. I couldn't fight them all, and Oriel knew it. He sent strong revenants with precise control at me, and then he cornered me. And then he said..." her voice trailed off, and I moved forward, standing near Rome. "I finally met him. I know exactly what he looks like, and now I know why he's been able to get within our wards."

I swallowed hard and leaned forward, unsure I wanted to hear the answer but knowing I needed to. That we all did.. "How, Rowen?"

"Because he's my brother."

It was as if she had thrown a rock into a pond, the rippling effect sending shock waves throughout us all. I blinked, trying to come to terms with what she had said, and yet it didn't sound so farfetched or crazy as it should have. No, things began to click into place, and nausea settled in.

"Before your father moved back to town."

Rowen met my gaze as the others gave us curious looks. I knew her secrets from when we had been younger. I knew much of the Ravenwood lore because I had been living in it for so long before the Christopher curse had come to fruition.

It was as if time stood still and we were teenagers again, discussing our families and what we thought would happen next. What we thought the darkness could ever be.

She looked at me then and pressed her lips together. "He's my half-brother. I don't know if my father ever actually knew him. I don't think so. But he's been out there all this time. He has an affinity for air just like I do, and the runes etched on his skin speak of a power that has been years in the making. He is a necromancer, and he is a Ravenwood. Older than me by a few years."

I let out another curse. "That doesn't make him the heir. You know that."

"He's older. By rights, he should be *the* Ravenwood."

"No, that's not how things work," Sage put in, and Rowen gave a hollow laugh.

"It's how it's always worked in the past. The eldest Ravenwood, the one with the most power, they were the ones in control of the coven."

I shook my head. "And yet, he's a necromancer. Therefore, he can't hold the title or the power to protect the town. You know it."

I'd never seen Rowen look as lost as she did now. If I had a soul, it would break in that moment. "Do I? I'm not strong enough. We know this. We know what this town is doing to me. It was like this even before you came back. I couldn't even leave the town boundaries for longer than an hour or I'd weaken right along with the town wards. And yes, we are stronger together, but would we have been stronger with him here?"

"Stop it," I lashed out, and she met my gaze, the air between us sizzling with her magic.

"Don't tell me what to do, Ash. You lost that right. No, then again, you never had it."

The snarl escaped before I could hold it back and I wasn't sure I wanted to at all. "Launch your barbs at me all you want, but you know that you're just scared."

"Stop it," she lashed.

"No, I will not. Yes, it's startling to realize that your father had a bastard out there, and yet, it happened. Just because Oriel has some magic that is similar does not mean he is *the* Ravenwood. He cannot be. He was not trained in the arts like you were. He has not given up so much of himself to protect this town. I don't even have a soul, Rowen, and I understand what sacrifices you've made for this damn town. Maybe if things had been different, he could have been by your side, but he would never have been *the* Ravenwood. He wants to corrupt. He wants power. We know this. We have heard it from his underlings, and now he was here showing why. We can fight back. Don't you understand that?"

"He has access to everything I do. I was so naïve to use my own blood with the wards, with the core, with everything. I used the power of Ravenwood to protect us, and now it's going to be what destroys us."

"Then use the power of the coven. Of the magic itself. Use the Christophers and the Princes. Use all of them. Not just Ravenwood. This town may bear your name, but you do not bear the responsibility alone of protecting it." I had never understood Rowen's need to do this alone and yet I knew she'd never listen to me. Not after all I'd done to her in the past.

"I agree with Ash," Laurel said, and Rowen's gaze shot to her, betrayed. "What? I am finally strong enough, so is Sage. We are here. To protect you."

I moved forward then, though I didn't touch her. She wouldn't want my touch anymore. "Don't you see that? We are here for each other. Let us know how we can help, damn it. I know the spells too. I have access to the same grimoire. We will protect this town, and we will make sure that Oriel cannot get to the power. That he cannot hurt any more of us."

"He's my brother," she whispered, and if I could feel like I should, I would break for her.

Instead, I narrowed my eyes at her words. "He is of blood, but he is so far gone he's not who you think he could be."

"You're saying he's a lost cause," Rowen whispered, meeting my gaze, and we weren't talking about Oriel any longer.

"He was a lost cause from the moment he took that step. We both know that."

"We need the coven," Sage put in, and I knew she was trying to break the tension between us—it would never work. That was the problem.

"Yes, the *coven*," I said drily.

"*All* of the coven," Laurel added.

Rowen narrowed her gaze. "You know it's been the three. That's what was foretold."

I threw my hands in the air and growled. "Fine. You three are the coven, I understand that, but what of earth? What of the fourth element? Don't you understand? It has always been air, water, and fire. But what of earth? Earth is the base for you to thrive. And until you understand that, Ravenwood could fall. It doesn't matter that your brother or whoever the hell he thinks he is will come in here with his own dark magic trying to go for the town. Until you use what is at your disposal, you will fail. And that's your problem, Rowen. You have the weight of the world on your shoulders, and yet you are the one that places it there. No one else." And with that, I walked away, leaving them behind, anger a familiar tome within my gut.

Walking away was what I did best, and it was time I remembered that.

CHAPTER
SIX

Oriel

Oriel's paws slid into the dirt before he stretched his back and shifted back into his human form. He tugged on the sleeves of his button-up shirt and grinned. It had been a *very* productive afternoon. Plans were falling into place almost too easily now.

Renee sat in a steel chair on the porch and smiled at him, though it didn't reach her eyes. He wasn't even aware if it had before she lost William, and he didn't care. All that mattered was that Renee was alive, and he could use her magic and grief for revenge against the coven. The angrier she was, the faster Ravenwood would fall. Of course, she would be the pawn he needed for the final spell, but she didn't know that.

"How is she?" Renee asked, her voice hoarse. The fire witch's vocal cords had been burned in the fire thanks to that phoenix bitch. Oriel had done his best.

"The first step has begun. They'll destroy themselves from the inside, the knowledge that has been hidden from them for so long now out in the open."

"And I'll be able to have her scalp?" Renee asked, and he laughed at the toxicity of it.

"Of course. You'll have your little phoenix and her little bird. I'll have the town and my sister. We need to ensure that the soulless one remains."

"Much like you?" Renee asked.

Oriel lifted a brow. "Much like me. As you can see, I have the power of the world in my hands because of who I am and the soul that was taken from me. When the other soulless one realizes whose side he should be on, we will finally be ready for the next step."

"Good. Because it is time, I'm done waiting."

"It will be time when I say it's time. Remember who's the winner here."

Renee let out a growl before she stood up and limped into the house.

Weak. She was weak. But Oriel needed her. Faith was gone, the one person he could truly trust, or at least as much as he trusted at all. With her gone, however, Oriel needed Renee. At least for as long as it took for the soulless one to come to his side. Together Ash and Oriel would destroy Ravenwood. It was foretold, after all.

Oriel rolled his shoulders back and walked into the home, the sounds of screaming abruptly dying off. He thought Renee was done with her little pet project, the lone panther that had tried to come to Ravenwood for help.

Poor Ravenwood didn't even realize that the shifters that were coming for help, weren't making it through the wards. Rowen would try to change those wards to make it so Ravenwoods couldn't enter as he had before, but she wasn't as strong as him. And once she realized that, the next step would continue.

And finally, Oriel would have Ravenwood. He would have his power.

And he would have the world.

CHAPTER
SEVEN

Rowen

"**M**agic mends while candles burn, sickness ends and health returns. Harm to none, this we decree. This is our will, so mote it be!" Magic sizzled up my arms, down my spine, and I let out a slow breath, allowing the rest of the spell do its work.

The cord that connected me to this particular ward pulsated just a bit as if it weren't sure it would be strong enough, but I knew it had to be. There wasn't going to be another option. So, I let in the magic and out the worry and doubt.

"That sizzled," Laurel said with a slight giggle, and I

looked over to see my best friend rolling her shoulders back and then shaking out her hands.

"We're getting stronger." Sage smiled softly and then pulled her hair back, loosely braiding it over one shoulder. "I mean, I feel like I'm getting stronger, so I hope I'm helping strengthen the wards more."

I nodded tightly and looked around my small garden, doing my best not to panic. Or at least not let the others know I was panicking.

Because the wards weren't getting more powerful, though, we *were* stronger. Our coven and the magic within our veins were growing leaps and bounds. Yet, something was wrong. And I knew what it was.

I had keyed the wards to my blood because I was the daughter's daughter's daughter of the Ravenwood.

I had keyed my Ravenwood blood to the town, thinking I was the final one. I had been so naïve, and yet, there wasn't anything I could do. Because our coven of three wasn't going to be strong enough. Not when Oriel had backdoor access to everything that came with the town's core and its protections.

"What's that look for?" Laurel asked as she moved in front of me, snapping me out of my thoughts.

"Nothing."

"No, you don't get to lie. We do not lie to each other. So, you're going to tell me what's wrong." She studied my face, and then her skin went impossibly pale. "It's not working," she whispered, her voice barely above a whisper.

"It is," I denied.

"No. It's not. It's not working. Yes, we're more powerful, yes Sage and I are putting more into the wards themselves, but we're missing something big. We have to be."

I shook my head, my magic waning. "You're not. It's not like that."

"Don't lie to us," Sage put in. "Lying will only hurt us in the end. Talk to us."

I met my coven's gazes, put my hands over my face, and screamed.

"Well, that's a new one," Laurel mumbled as she moved forward and pulled my hands from my face. "Talk to us."

"I made a mistake. I did this all wrong. Don't you understand that? Oriel has the ability to get through our wards like a hot knife through butter. That's why he's been able to send the revenants as he has. That's why he was able to shove Faith through the wards. Why Faith was able to get to not only Penelope but to Trace. Even Alden. She was able to twist his mind and his insecurities into having him betray his brothers. All of that. Because Oriel could go through our wards sight unseen. Because I thought I was alone. And I was wrong."

A tear-filled Sage moved forward and wiped my face. "You are not to blame for Trace, for Alden, or for my aunt's death. Do not blame yourself."

"How can I not blame myself when they're dead? They're gone. And if I had used any other spell, he wouldn't have gotten through."

"Bullshit."

I turned at Laurel's words, my eyes wide. "Excuse me?"

"That is bullshit. You didn't do anything wrong. You added to the wards of Ravenwood. You tied your soul to this town in order to protect the power that lies beneath it and its people. When I couldn't put forth any extra power, and when Sage wasn't here because of a spell that kept her away—Oriel's spell might I add—you nearly died for this town. And it wasn't Oriel draining the power. It was the town itself. Because we weren't a true coven. But now we are. So, we're going to fucking find a way to make it work."

"If you want to lay blame, why don't you lay it on me? I wasn't here." Sage looked at me, her jaw tight.

I shook my head. "A spell pushed you away. It didn't let you realize your birthright."

Sage didn't back down. "We could blame my mother then. Or the spell that took my mother away. Or maybe I wasn't strong enough to begin with, and that's why I couldn't fight the compulsions to stay out of Ravenwood and realize that magic was real."

I blinked. "Sage, you know that's not true. Why would you even think that?"

"You blame yourself for what you think is failing and are continuing to blame yourself for nearly dying because of a curse of not of your own making. All of us would be stupid to blame ourselves for these circumstances. We are doing what we can and trying to save this town and the people that we love. Don't make a mockery of that by blaming yourself."

"I love when she gets all feisty like that. It sounds like she's of the fire, rather than me."

"Water can drown, and douse your fire, so watch yourself." Sage looked so prim and proper as she said it, I couldn't help the smile drawn to my face.

We stood in a circle, the three of us, my coven, my sisters, my fate.

I loved them with every ounce of my being, and yet I was so afraid I wasn't strong enough.

"We need to do another spell," I said, after a minute. "To firm our defenses, to put a protection spell around the core."

"I know, we said we would. We'll do it now." Laurel looked at me as she spoke, her gaze unwavering. "You're our sister. We're not going to let Oriel poison your mind. He may be blood, but he's not family. He's nothing but an egotistical little prick who didn't get what he wanted as a child. And while part of me will feel bad that maybe he wasn't loved as a kid, that doesn't excuse what he's done. He has gone completely to dark magic. He has tainted his soul and probably even ripped it away completely." Her eyes widened as I swallowed hard.

"I don't think he has a soul. I think he's gone past even

dark necromancers and doesn't even have the tainted part left."

"It's not like Ash," Sage added quickly, and I looked at her.

"What are you talking about?"

"You're making comparisons. Or he will. He is not like Ash. Ash had a curse rip his soul from him. And we're going to find a way to bring it back."

I didn't tell them that Ash and I had already discussed it, that we knew the only way to make it happen would be the same way that we had broken the curse for Laurel.

Only there wasn't a path out for Ash. There wasn't a bond of sibling and mate. Not like with Laurel. Because Ash and I had had our bond broken, there was no coming back from that. To bring Ash's soul back, I was afraid it would kill him. And, despite everything, I wasn't able to do that.

Maybe I was the weak one.

"What aren't you saying?" Laurel whispered.

I shook my head. "We need to do the spell."

"Rowen. Stop putting everything onto your own shoulders and hiding. Talk to us."

I lifted my chin, fear making my words sharper than I intended. "Talk to your brother. I don't have it in me right now. Okay?"

She met my gaze again, then nodded tightly.

"Okay. I'll let you have that. For now. But I'm going to talk to my brother."

"That's fine. But we need to protect the core."

"And we will."

"*Magic mends while candles burn, sickness ends and health returns. Harm to none, this we decree. Protect what is ours. What is right. Bright forth the magic that is might. This is our will, so mote it be!*"

A wave of dizziness smashed into me, and I staggered back, my feet sliding in the mud, and I fell. My hands hit the wet earth, the culmination of our elements, and I swallowed hard, my teeth chattering.

Laurel and Sage were at my side in an instant, both trying to hold me up, to keep me steady, and I pushed at them, needing air.

"I'm fine. I just need a moment to breathe."

"You're not fine. I have never seen a spell hit you like that," Laurel whispered, her eyes wide with fear.

As that fear echoed within my own body, I didn't blame her just then.

"I'm calling Rome," Sage said as she pulled away, digging her phone out of her pocket.

I reached for her, to tell her not to bother, but one look at Laurel and I pressed my lips together in a scowl.

"Don't. We three here are doing our magic because of who we are together. The only reason they weren't here to begin with is that they were dealing with the dustup and cleanup from the last attack."

I nodded, understanding. Rome and Jaxton, while alpha and wing leader of their respective shifters, were also the cleanup for Ravenwood. Whatever magic couldn't hold back or hide, they would cleanup. Sometimes it was broken windows. Sometimes it was a shattered home. It had made me ill to think that, at one point, they had had to help clear gravesites because of what Oriel and his ilk had done with the revenants. However, we used magic and an ancient spell from one of my ancestor's grimoires to protect the earth and land that those graves stood on. No longer could anyone from Ravenwood be used in that manner, unless we couldn't get to them first.

It sometimes haunted my dreams to think that anyone around us could be killed and then used for Oriel's gain. Sometimes Frank, our old jaguar friend, would limp towards me in my dreams, half-shifter, half-human, growling an inhuman noise and trying to rip my throat out. Other times it would be Esmeralda or Esther, the elderly witch with only a single drop of power. She could do nothing other than sense who she was, and yet she tried to put her life on the line every single day to protect this town. But, in my dreams, she came at me, a shade rather than a revenant. Her body decayed, but someone used her soul and twisted it for their own magic.

In reality, Esther had used that single drop of magic to help me fortify the wards. The same as every witch in town—anyone with any hereditary power that wasn't even power. They might not be coven because to do so would kill them. The draw on their magic would strip their life force so it wouldn't be safe, but when I needed them, they had been there for me. They had been my special coven, and I would fight and die to protect them.

"They're on their way," Sage said after a moment, and Laurel nodded.

"Good, that means I don't have to call them," a familiar deep voice said from behind me, and I stood up, hating the fact that I was covered in mud and sweat and fatigue.

Ash lifted his chin and glared at us. "You should not be doing magic like this without a spotter. I told you I would be your base, and yet you're still doing this? Look at yourselves. Look at Rowen. It is draining her; can't you see that?"

"Ash," Laurel snapped.

He held out his hand. "I don't need to have a soul to realize what it's doing to her. Every time you use magic to protect this town, it is draining the life from her. You can see the dark circles under her eyes, the fact that she can't even run up the stairs like she used to. She still fights with everything that she has, but what is left? We need to do something. You know this."

My heart twisted and I let out a breath. "What? What is there to do?"

"Use the spell," he spat.

"What spell?" Sage asked, her voice low.

"The spell to bring my soul back."

Laurel shoved at me, her eyes narrowing to daggers. "There's a spell to bring my brother back?" she yelled, her voice cracking. "And you didn't tell me? You, of all people, you didn't tell me?"

I shook my head, tears threatening to fall. "It will kill him. It's even worse than the spell that brought you back."

"And I came back as a phoenix."

"And you killed Jaxton to make it happen," I shouted before I put my hand over my mouth, shocked I'd even said the words.

Laurel staggered back as if I had hit her, and maybe I had. She shook her head, tears freely falling now. "You're right. I killed the one person that I loved. And then I died too. But fate had a way. Fate has to have a way." She looked between Ash and me. "You two are mates."

"No. We're not."

The fact that I said it simultaneously as Ash wasn't lost on me, and once again, my heart shattered into a thousand pieces, the unending pain almost a cool balm to the ache in my soul. At least it was something familiar.

"You're just lying to yourself because you're hurting, and I understand it. But if there's a spell to bring my brother back, then we need to do it."

"You say that as if I'm not standing right here," Ash mumbled.

"Don't use semantics on me, you know it. You are not the Ash that you once were, and while I still love this Ash, I want my brother. Ravenwood needs my brother." She paused, another tear falling. "Rowen needs you, Ash."

"That's enough," I snapped. "The spell will kill him. I

need to find something else, something stronger to anchor him here. Because I'm not it." I hadn't meant to say the last part, but now the words were out there and there was no taking them back.

I was truly afraid that whatever bond Ash and I once held, the memory of the bond that I buried deep within myself, wouldn't have the strength to tether him to this world. Worse, I knew that my body might break under the weight of that bond and the bond to the town itself.

I wasn't enough.

Even though I'd spent my life trying to be so.

"Then let us read the spell," Sage put in, breaking me out of my thoughts. "Hiding it and pretending it isn't a problem isn't making things easier."

"I know. I know." I let out a sigh. "We've been so worried about everything else I've let it fall to the wayside."

"Thank you for the confidence and help there," Ash said dryly, and I flipped him off.

"Shut up. Just shut up."

"Anything you say, witch. As always."

Jaxton and Rome ran up at that moment, their eyes wide as they took in the scene. We looked a mess, and as I could taste the tension in the air, I knew that the shifters would be able to as well.

Rome cleared his throat. "I'd ask what we missed, but I'm a little afraid to."

"We can start with the fact that every time that we use

magic these days to protect this town, it's slowly killing Rowen. Again." Sage raised her chin as I let out a breath, my hands clammy once more. "I know that we can protect the people by evacuating them or doing something else, but that's not all, is it?" Sage asked, and I shook my head.

"It's not. Because Ravenwood lies above the core of magic. It was the magic of the coven that first grew it, this power and pulse of raw magic that is untrained and unheard of. With each passing generation, more magic from shifter and fae and witch alike has blended into this power. It's not unstable. It won't destroy the earth if unchecked. It's not like that."

"But it's those who hold the power, who dig into it. They're the ones that will be corrupted," Ash added.

"Maybe. Or maybe the core will just explode, and nothing will happen. Maybe it'll dissipate throughout all of the world, the magic going back the way it should due to the law of thermodynamics, but we don't know. And the fact that we don't know means we need to keep it away from Oriel. It is my duty as the final Ravenwood." I stumbled over the words and frowned. "Or it was my duty as my father's daughter. I suppose I'm not the last Ravenwood any longer."

"Semantics," Ash put in. "However, you need the coven of three with your anchor. And I'm not talking about the tattoo etched on your skin." Ash raised his chin. "We need my soul back, and though most of me doesn't understand why, the part of me screaming is louder than ever."

I frowned, confused. Ash had never spoken like that before to me, and I didn't understand what he was saying. From the looks on everyone else's faces, neither did they.

Ash merely shook his head and didn't elaborate. "I need my soul, and we need to find this Oriel and end this once and for all. Ravenwood needs us, or at least it needs you. So, let's make that happen."

I looked at him then, and at my friends, and as a pulse of magic hit the wards, just a testing breeze, I staggered again, this time falling. I knew Ash held me as I fell, but I didn't care. I just let the magic fade, and I went under.

This darkness was far more peaceful than the darkness trying to murder us.

At least that's what I told my subconscious.

And then, I slept.

EIGHT

Ash

I wasn't cut off from emotion. I was merely cut off from everything else. That was something I routinely needed to remind myself of. I was not a revenant. Nor was I a shade. But I was the consequences of my own making. Or perhaps the consequences of my ancestors making.

I sat back in my chair, swirling the amber liquid in my glass as I looked around the home that Laurel had helped me build after I had moved away. Some part of me hadn't wanted to leave Ravenwood behind completely, and I didn't know if that was the need for the prophecy or unfinished business. Or perhaps a tiny part of me always wanted to rule in every place I was. I had the penthouse in Manhattan, the mansion in Malibu. Another mountain cabin in Aspen. And a plot of land in Tennessee where I was building a few places for a homestead. In addition to those, I had a few places around the world I could travel to easily, though I'd spent most of my time near Ravenwood —near Rowen. Not that I lived in any of those places these days. No, this relatively smaller home compared to my others, even though it was the largest home in Raven-wood, was my roof over my head for the time being.

It was two stories, with a full attic and a basement. It was far too large for a single person, and Laurel had rolled her eyes every time that she mentioned it. A couple of the hawk shifters from Jaxton's wing were caretakers for it and helped keep it updated and clean. Helped kept the pipes warm in the icy winters and helped air it out during springs and summers. They planted in the gardens, although I knew that part of it was Laurel as well. Though she was a fire witch, and I was of earth, my sister was always good with plants. Perhaps not as good as Rowen, but all witches had an affinity for something.

Take Sage and her baking. She had been infusing part of herself in her food, a warm magic that had come from within, far before she had realized who she was and where she had come from.

Though Oriel's own magic work had pulled Sage away

from us for far longer than we had ever even thought, it hadn't been able to hide her forever.

I had to wonder exactly how long Oriel had even known of Sage's existence. After all, Sage's mother had left Ravenwood as a teenager, and Oriel was younger than that. Perhaps the prophecy itself had taken its own twist to that magic, and Oriel had only added substance to the curse.

Many of Ravenwood's magical left town. Especially when they realized that their magic was never going to be like Rowen's. Or even Penelope's. Penelope had been a gentle witch with a slight power but could only really use what was inside her for spells Rowen wrote for her. She didn't even have a pure affinity like the rest of us.

But Sage's aunt had given her life to protect this town and her niece.

Other witches stayed, even though they didn't have the power. Although, in reality, as one of the only ones of us who had actually been around the world, the witches that moved to Ravenwood possessed far more power than many who claimed to be of the craft.

I took a sip of my whiskey, letting the fiery burn slide down my throat as I focused. I needed to speak with Rowen. Again. And yet, I couldn't get the image of her passing out in my arms out of my mind. I felt nothing for that woman. And yet, that screaming part of me couldn't help but want to ensure her safety. If she died, then the town died. It was my legacy. And that was all the rational-ization I needed in order for her to live.

A spell would break me, and yet, was I not already broken? Was I not already the shattered remains of that glass that had fractured long before I had even fallen for Rowen?

Because I had known something would happen. That the curse would enact. Every curse within my family broke something. And it intensified with each passing generation. Nearly losing my sister was a perfect example of that. The man with the soul had been such a selfish prick that he had let Rowen fall for him knowing that something could end him quickly. How was that any better than a man without a soul?

And yet I knew, in order to complete the magic and to ensure that my place in the coven was at its base and at its strength, I needed my soul. My magic was faulty without it. That was simple science. Simple rationale. I didn't need a soul to feel. I didn't need a soul for Rowen.

I needed it to be the best man I could be. Because of the magic itself. Not because of the man I saw in the mirror, nor the woman who would never speak to me.

But something was happening with her, something beyond the wards, or her exhaustion from fighting the revenants. Something she was hiding from us. And as a man who had hidden things far too long, who thrived in those secrets, I recognized it. And yet, I knew it wasn't enough.

I had burned my way through Ravenwood, not caring about those I slashed and pummeled along the way.

The only ones that had been left standing had been the ones I had hurt the most, and yet here they were, continuing to fight for Ravenwood. I could do the same because I was strong enough. Soul or no soul, I was that man. And others needed to understand that.

It was not my fault that one of Sage's ancestors had fallen for one of mine. She had fallen for a man in my line, with so much innocent strength that when she had found that he hadn't loved her back, she had broken in grief, and the power lashed out at the Christopher line. It had been an unknowing action, an action that she hadn't meant to take. And yet, the wake of that fall had been a catastrophe for my family. With each passing generation, the power embedded within the curse sent more and more of us to our deaths and sent more and more magic firing through our veins to the point that we combusted. My sister had literally burned alive because of a young girl's love for another.

I lost my soul like a dark witch, like a necromancer, because a young girl had fallen in love.

The Prince witch hadn't lost her soul. No, she had lived to see the curse become what it was. To watch the core of the town intensify the curse because they were the ones that were building to begin with.

They took the magic of their coven, the magic of their family lines, combined it along with the other species, and built this town. They protected, and they cared, and they created a power that nobody could control. A power that others craved and demanded.

And now we were the final defense—that final line.

And I needed my soul back, despite the fact that I wanted nothing to do with it.

Because I needed to have nothing to do with it.

I downed the rest of my drink, preparing for what I must do, when the familiar spicy scent hit my nostrils. I stood up, setting the empty glass next to me as Rowen walked into my home as if she owned the place. I had locked it, of course, had used my own wards to keep others out, but Rowen had always been able to slide through my wards, just like I had been able to hers.

Because the man I was had been hers, after all.

"Hello there." I tilted my head as I studied her face, wondering why she was here. And wondering why she called to me even though I knew it had to be an echo of a bond that once was.

"You're so angry I can hear your screaming from here."

I snorted and then moved to lift my glass.

"Drinking alone while the fire rages seems far more warlock of you than I ever imagined."

My lips twitched. "I always hated the old-fashioned name for male witches. I'm a witch. A soulless one, but a witch. A warlock is one step closer to the darkness. At least, that's what my father used to say." I grabbed the glass, picked up the decanter, and poured myself three fingers of whiskey. I did the same to another glass and handed it to her.

She raised a brow at the amount of liquid. "Getting me drunk for this conversation, are you?"

I snorted, but she took the glass anyway. "I don't need you drunk for anything, Rowen. You've always known what you wanted to say and what you want in life. No amount of drinking or magic flowing in those veins of yours is going to change that."

Her lips lifted in a slight smile before she shook her head and downed the whiskey in one gulp.

I winced at the look on her face and sighed, sipping the rest of mine. "I'll have you know, you only drink it that quickly when you have the cheap stuff. This is the good stuff. This is what you sip."

"Well, I was never good at whiskey, even though I keep it in my house. You remember that."

I snorted. "Oh yes, I do. What were two sixteen-year-olds drinking cheap whiskey to do?"

She narrowed her eyes. "I remember exactly what we did that night."

"The magic that we produced was quite powerful."

A wry smile played on her lips. "Maybe it had to do with the whiskey."

I shook my head and sipped my drink before I set it down again. "Should you really be drinking now that I think about it?"

"Excuse me?" she asked, her voice so affronted it made

me smile.

"You nearly passed out how many times today? Or should I even use the word *nearly*? You fell into my arms. Swooned like a Regency woman with her corset too tight. One who couldn't eat for the entire day because she had to fit in that dress so she could be noticed by her suitor. Just bland lemonade and little cookies that taste like flour and butter."

"How many Regency romances have you been reading, Ash?" she asked with a laugh.

"I wanted to know what Laurel saw in Jaxton. What Sage saw in Rome. I wanted to know what I was missing."

She looked like I had struck her, and she set down her empty glass. "You're a bastard, do you know that?"

"No, my parents were married when I was conceived and born. I'm an asshole, though. You've known that. I was an asshole before the little incident with the Christopher curse."

"The little incident. Well, I guess that's why I'm here."

"Are you finally going to deem yourself prepared for the spell that I know you're strong enough for?"

"I've always been strong enough for it, Ash. That was never the problem. You know that."

"Then give me my fucking soul," I spat.

Her eyes widened, and I cursed under my breath.

"I haven't heard you sound so passionate in, well, let's just say it's been a long time."

"I haven't sounded this passionate since what? I last

fucked you? I remember, Rowen. I remember it all. Just because there's a veil over it now that makes me not understand it doesn't erase the memories. I remember how you taste, how you feel. I remember the way you blush when you come. I remember it all."

"Fuck you," she growled.

"I think we were talking about me fucking you, but I digress. You're welcome to fuck me any time you want, Rowen. Maybe that would help lighten the blow. Help relieve that tension. Clearly alcohol isn't doing it. Maybe you just need a quick lay."

I should have expected the slap. I deserved it.

Rowen moved back, looked down at her hand, and began to shake. "I don't know why. I know you say these words to antagonize me. To bring out my magic. I know it's because the person that I know is gone. And yet, I've never hit another human being other than in self-defense. Except for you. What kind of monster does that make me? I'm the one with the soul, and yet I lash out."

I moved to her without thinking, cupping her face. "I'm the one that brings out the worst in you. I know that. And I don't know why I react the way that I do. It makes no sense, don't you understand? I don't have a connection to this world, and yet I yell at you, I push at you. I need you to be there, and I don't understand why. Why is that, Rowen?"

She was so close to me, my hands on her, and when

she slid her palms down my arms, I let her pull me away. "I don't understand, Ash."

"I don't either. But we know that in order to keep the town safe, to keep the core of Ravenwood protected, I need my soul."

"And if you survive somehow, are you going to be able to face the man in the mirror after everything that you've done?"

"What have I done?"

"You've lied, you've cheated, you've stolen, you've done so much in the name of power, and yet you still want the remorse?"

I raised my chin, memories of the past decade or so of what I had done to become the man in power. The laws I'd broken, the lines I'd crossed. But there were a few lines that I had never crossed. And she needed to understand that.

"I was never with a person who was unwilling. I never cheated on another because I was never with another in that way. I was never the horrific person you think I am. I've never murdered. I've never beaten a man because I wanted what he had. I just took it. The only ones I fight are the ones who come after my town. Who come after my sister. That is because I cannot lose. That is what is ingrained in me as a Christopher. It doesn't take a soul for that. So, yes. I have lied, and I have cheated laws, and I have broken them. I have stolen, and I have been the worst sort of person to get where I am. And I will have to live with that. The man who I used to be will have to live with that. But we need to protect this town. So let me."

"And what about me?" she whispered, and I moved forward, cupping her face. She was so small in my hands, my thumb over her lips, my fingers grasping her chin and her neck.

"What about you, Rowen?"

"Can you still look at me, knowing what you've done?"

"I'm looking at you now."

And then I did what I shouldn't. But then again, I was an asshole. Who was here to stop me?

I kissed her.

I groaned at the taste of whiskey on her tongue, an aphrodisiac. I tightened my hold on her neck, arched her chin up, and devoured her.

She didn't push me away. Instead, she clung to me, raking her nails down my back.

I bit her lip, hard enough to sting, and kissed her again, running my hands down her body. I tugged on her shirt, pulling it over her head. The ripping fabric echoed within the room, and I didn't care. She stood in a bra and a skirt, and I shoved her skirt up and pushed her against the door. Her eyes widened, but I didn't care.

She didn't push me away, didn't tell me to stop. So, I didn't.

Instead, I shoved her thighs apart, lifted her up, and ground against her. She was hot against my jean-clad cock, and I ground harder, rotating my hips ever so slightly, so she hummed along me. I kissed her hard again, then pulled her head to the side and latched on her neck, sucking and biting. She shivered, the magic around us swirling. The air pulsated, books were tossed off the shelf, the fire raged from the air swirling. The couch behind me lifted, glass shattered, and I still kissed her, still needed her. She shoved her hands between us, undoing my belt buckle and my jeans, and then she held me in her hand, hot and ready. I glared down at her, and she sent daggers right back to me, but I positioned myself and shoved into her, hard and fast, and she screamed my name, and a part of me broke.

But not the part I expected.

"More," she whispered. "Please."

"Beg, my witch. That's how I like it."

"Bastard."

"Always."

Yours.

I didn't say that part.

She arched for me, and I ripped her bra away, latching onto her nipples to suck and play with her breasts. I pumped in and out of her, the house shaking from the power of my earth magic mixing with her air. I knew she would have bruises on her back, maybe even around her neck, but then again, I felt the blood seeping down my back from her long nails, and knew we both needed this, wanted this.

It was rough, and it was harsh, and it was more than anything that I knew she had ever had before.

This was nothing like who we had once been.

And yet, I knew it was everything.

I was so angry, and I didn't know why.

And I knew she was angry too.

And when I slid my hand between her, playing with her clit, she came, and so I pulled out of her, going to my knees quickly. I sucked on her cunt, lapping up her juices, before I speared her with two fingers, looking up at her as she stood there, a torn bra, her skirt rucked up to her waist, her gray eyes dark.

I fucked her with my fingers, lapping at her clit, the sounds we were making too loud for words or anything else. Magic swirled around us, shaking the house, sounding as if we were in a wind tunnel. When she came on my hand again, I pulled my fingers out and slid my cock through her folds before I dove deep inside her. She screamed my name, and I slid my wet fingers in her mouth. She sucked on them, her eyes wide but dark with need, and when I kissed her again, I tasted her, I tasted us.

And then I was coming, the roar bellowing from my throat as if it had been ripped from me. I filled her, both of us shaking, as I looked down at her and let out an aching breath.

"Well then," I whispered, trying to hear my voice above the screaming in my head and of the magic around us.

She looked at me then, her eyes still dark with need, and she cupped my face.

"We'll get your soul back, Ash. I promise."

And yet, I felt nothing. I couldn't.

I had lost everything.

And now I was going to have to face the consequences of tonight, of yesterday, and of tomorrow.

CHAPTER
NINE

Ash

Vines erupted from the earth, wrapping their tendrils around my ankles, my thighs, my wrists, my chest. They pulled me deeper, and I fought, twisting side to side, trying to break free of the vines. They dug in, their thorns cutting into my skin, my blood seeping into the earth below me. I fisted my hands at my side, trying to twist them up slightly so I could face my palms to the sky and call forth my magic, but the vines strengthened their hold, and the earth began to open up, swallowing me. Dirt and sod fell into my mouth as I screamed, as the pressure of the ground around me began to suffocate me, pressing in, my blood mixing with that of the soil and the earth's own life.

Dirt covered my face, and then there was nothing, only my frantic breaths as I choked on the earth itself, on the magic I could not hold.

And I screamed.

I shot out of bed, my chest heaving as I tried to focus on the here and now, not the empty cavern screaming inside me and the dreams that tended to haunt me.

"Fuck," I growled and wiped my hand over my sweaty face.

I should've known that the dreams would come back, the ones where I was suffocating and being killed by my own magic and yet unable to actually perform any of my own spells and protect myself.

The dreams that haunted me usually revolved around being buried alive, a fear I had never had when I had possessed my soul. Yet, it seemed that with the curse came a new worry that I hadn't realized would be an issue.

If the dreams didn't throw me to the wolves or suffocate me, they did so to Rowen. Or Laurel. Or Trace. Or Rome. Or Jaxton. I had also had one where Sage had been buried alive, but only recently, since I'd gotten to know her after the world had thrown her for a loop.

More often than not, though, it was me or Rowen. I wasn't sure what I was supposed to do with that information. It wasn't like I could wake myself up from the nightmare. Even if it felt like sometimes I could be a third party to witness my own death, I couldn't scream myself awake. I had to witness my failings and final assignations.

And then sometimes I would wake up wanting to throw up. Just now, my stomach turned, and I swallowed hard, reminding myself that I was strong. I could do this. And I didn't need to vomit because I was awake. I was alive. And today was the day I was going to retain my soul.

It didn't seem real, and yet it was what I needed. Not because I wanted it. And that was the problem, wasn't it? I didn't want my soul. I needed it. It was a failure not to have one because I needed the strength. So here I was, pretending once again. And today would be the day that I dreamed of myself dying, rather than Rowen. More often than not these days, it was solely Rowen. But today was the day. Where everything changed, where I would most likely die, and yet, at least I was trying something. At least we were trying to move forward—something we hadn't been doing in far too long because of the consequences. And because Oriel had held the upper hand for far too long. No longer. Now we would be the ones in control.

At least, that was what I was telling myself in this instance.

"Knock knock," a voice said from the front room.

I sighed, got out of bed, and quickly pulled on a pair of pants before my sister walked into the back room.

"I like that your master bedroom's on the first floor. You still have that view and don't have to deal with stairs all by your lonesome, old man."

I let out a slight growl at her as I shoved past her and into the kitchen.

"Thanks for putting pants on for me. That's something I do not need to see."

"Is there a reason you're so perky this morning?"

"I brought banana nut muffins from Sage. She made them especially for us early this morning since she couldn't sleep."

I raised a brow at her and made myself a cup of coffee.

"And how does she know that we like banana nut?"

"Because she's one of my best friends. Of course, she knows."

"I suppose that makes sense."

"I don't know if banana nut is your favorite anymore. For all I know, you're a blueberry streusel man."

My lips twitched despite myself, and I handed over my cup of coffee to her before making one of my own.

She smiled softly and took a sip. "Sometimes, there are little parts of you that remind me of the person that I miss. The person that used to be there."

I tilted my head and studied her.

"Do you think I'll be so much different when I get my soul back?"

"Are you seriously asking me that?" she asked with a laugh.

"I voiced the words, did I not?" I took the coffee mug from beneath the brewer, added my cream and sugar, and took a sip. The aroma hit my nostrils, and I had to wonder if it would be different once I had my soul. I could barely remember what things tasted like or felt like before things had been irrevocably altered. And I had to wonder why I cared just then.

"Things are going to change, Ash. You know that." She studied my face, frowning. "Why are you doing this if you don't think that there will be any change at all?"

I took another sip of my coffee then set the mug down.

"I'm doing this because the town needs me."

"Doesn't that seem like a perplexing statement for a man without a soul? Why do you care?"

I frowned. "I don't."

"Are you telling me, or are you telling yourself?"

"It's what I told Rowen last night." I hadn't meant to say the words. My sister always left me off-kilter. As if she were speaking to the man that I once was, rather than the man that I was now.

"She was here? Well, that makes sense. She called late last night to let us know the spell would be happening today, after all."

I shrugged, took another sip of my coffee, and Laurel's mug clattered to the counter.

"You slept with her."

I raised a brow. "Is that something I should be talking to my little sister about?"

"You asshole. You can't just sleep with Rowen."

"Why not? We were good at it. We always were."

Laurel ran her hands through her fiery red hair and

began to pace my kitchen. "Because when you get your soul back, you're going to have to deal with the things that you've done. I love you, Ash. You're my brother, and I will always love you. But you have made poor decisions. You have hurt people. And I know it's not truly your fault, and yet it still is. You need to take responsibility for what you've done. And sleeping with Rowen? You're going to hurt her. More than you already have."

"She was of sound mind and body when she made the decision to sleep with me. I did not force her."

Laurel must have heard the growl in my voice because her eyes widened. "I know you wouldn't."

"Really? For a man with no soul, you sure give me morals."

"Because you're not evil. You're not a necromancer. You're not a dark practitioner. Despite everything, you have never used your magic to hurt. There's always been some part of you holding back. So no, I don't think you would have forced Rowen. But I think it was a fucking messy decision."

I shrugged, downed the rest of my coffee. "Perhaps. But I suppose the new and improved Ash will have to deal with it on his own. I need to shower before we go. One must be clean for a new soul after all."

"Ash. I love you."

"I know you do."

I saw the hurt on her face that I didn't say it back, but

the thing was, I didn't love her. I appreciated my sister. I knew she was important.

But I didn't love her. Just like I didn't love Rowen.

And I supposed if the spell didn't kill me first, I'd have to come to terms with that inevitability.

WE STOOD in Rowen's home, the wards around the property stronger than before. I could feel them keyed not to Rowen's blood but to the coven itself. Which was good, as Oriel had proven that he could get through Rowen's wards previously.

We were not alone as a coven. Instead, Rowen had brought others, surprising me.

"Thank you, Frank, for coming," Rowen said as she hugged the old jaguar.

The man grinned and leaned back against the wall, folding his muscled arms over his chest. He might be older, but he still looked like he could break somebody with his pinky. He also wasn't as fast as he used to be, but other than a hawk at full speed, he could outrun anyone here. He was a fighter, and he was a power. He was a lone jaguar, without a pack, without family, but he was power. Was that why he was here? Or was it to control me if this didn't go well?

Aspen was also there, a frown on his face as he studied the spell books behind Rowen's table. He had his hands in his pockets and looked far more casual than I had ever seen him.

Nelle wasn't here, but I knew that she was still recuperating within the fae lands. She had died, not almost died. She *had* died. But because it was a spell, she was able to come back because of her bond with Aspen. Rome and Jaxton were there as well, frowning at me as they studied everyone else in the room.

"Are we ready to go then?" I asked as I looked at the others, and they turned to Rowen. She rolled her shoulders back, and I realized then I hadn't spoken a word to her since she had walked out of my house. Since I had pulled out of her, and she'd used her glamour to clean herself up. I had ripped the clothing from her and hadn't even been able to offer her anything else to wear because she had been self-sufficient enough to take care of it on her own.

Because that was Rowen. The person who could always do things on her own.

"Yes, we're ready. There'll be two spells back-to-back. One to pull on the power of the core of the town."

"What? Are you sure that's safe?" Aspen asked as he walked forward, a frown on Frank's face as he leaned forward as well.

Rowen nodded and pressed her lips together. "It's the only way we can do this. We need Ash to have his soul so we can cement the coven and keep us strong enough to defeat Oriel. We don't have the luxury of using dark magic and tainting our own presence in order to fight back with Oriel. He is stronger than us as we are now. But with Ash, with the four elements, we will be able to fight. Alongside the fae and alongside the shifters. We will be strong enough. But we need the fourth element."

Aspen looked between Rowen and me after she spoke. "Is this safe then? I didn't even know you could access the core like that."

"It's as safe as we're going to be," Sage said with a sigh. "We'll be here to anchor Rowen, so the magic doesn't get out past these wards. So, we don't lure any unsuspecting revenants or dark magic users, or someone who doesn't even realize what it is that they're going towards."

Laurel continued. "We'll be here to protect the coven, and you will be here with your own magic, with your own power, to cement us. To keep us in the present."

"Because the second spell will be to pull Ash's soul from the curse itself and shove it back into his body. It's not going to be easy." She looked at me. "And it's not going to be painless."

I shrugged, knowing that the nonchalance was probably an act for everyone else. "It wasn't painless to lose my soul. I suppose it's only right that it won't be so to gain it back."

Rowen met my gaze, and I couldn't read her. I couldn't tell if this was what she wanted or what she was resigned to do. Maybe I'd be able to tell soon.

"There could be consequences," Aspen began, and we all looked to him.

"We know he could die, but I don't know what else to do," Rowen answered.

Aspen nodded. "I'm sure you're aware of that. But the core of the town contains not just magics of the witches that created our safety. It also has the power within it of the shifters and the fae and those that we don't even know. If you're not careful, something else could get out."

Ice trickled up my spine. "Then we have you here to make sure it doesn't."

The fae king met my eyes and nodded. "I will do what I have to in order to protect this town."

I heard the threat, as did Rome since the bear alpha growled, but I held up my hand. "Thank you, Aspen. If this doesn't work and my soullessness takes a new edge, I trust you to do what the others won't."

"Ash," Laurel spat, but it was Frank who spoke up.

"I'll help the king here. It'll destroy me, but rather me than your best friends and sister."

Tears were falling down Sage's cheeks as she leaned into her mate, and the old jaguar met the fae king's gaze. They both nodded and turned to me.

"Thank you."

It seemed odd to be thanking two men who were ready to kill me, but there wasn't another option. I was doing this for Ravenwood. Therefore, I needed to be strong enough to let go.

"Let's get started then," Rowen put in, as if we hadn't just marked me for death in case something went wrong.

They circled me as I sat on top of the Ravenwood symbol, my legs crossed and my shirt off. My anchors flowed as if a wind blew through the leaves, the tall trees reaching for something they couldn't name. Of course, I knew who that was and who blew the breeze. It wasn't my anchor. It was Rowen's. That connection there, despite everything.

"We the coven must circle him, with the other four behind us, keeping us steady."

"Then let's do it," Jaxton whispered, his voice stone, and I knew he was hiding what he was feeling. Because this could be the end. Finally, this could be the end.

"We're going to pull on the core, but we need to keep the magic centered within the circle here. If any gets out, Aspen, you need to stop us."

Aspen nodded as Rowen rolled her shoulders back again.

"Okay, here we go. Like we practiced."

She met my gaze, swallowed hard. "As we practiced," she repeated, her voice a whisper.

I nodded tightly. "I trust you."

Her eyes filled, but then she blinked the tears away, and I didn't know if that had been the right thing to say or not.

"*Magic mends while empires fall, sickness ends and health*

returns. Bright forth the power that is of thee. This is our will, so mote it be!"

The walls shook, the windows rattled. The wind whirled, the fire in the fireplace sprung up. The water in the vases around us burbled, and the ground beneath the house and around us shook.

Power surged, and I sucked in a breath as I looked around the circle at the glowing light emanating from the three witches. Their hair blew in an unseen wind, their eyes wide, their mouths parted, as the core of Ravenwood was opened.

Jaxton and Rome muttered things under their breath, their hands on their mate's shoulders, keeping them braced. Rowen had no brace. And yet she was standing tall, strength personified. Aspen and Frank prowled around the circle, their own inner power keeping the core's magic contained. I hadn't known exactly how they would be able to help, but it was as if this moment had been foretold, and this was exactly what needed to happen.

"Now his soul," Rowen began, and I looked at her gaze, and the inner screaming in my mind intensified, drowning out all others.

"We call on the ancestors to hear our plea.
For the soul taken was of earth and of peace.
Break the foundation of what was past.
Bring forth the forsaken before the thought that was last.
Shatter the remains of those bound in salvation.

Hear the words of those who call you mother and bring back the life that was once freely given.

For it is spoken.

So mote it be."

A knife dug into my chest, carving out my heart, my lungs, my tissues, and my bones. Fire slammed into my back, searing my flesh, the smell too much to bear as burning hair and molten flesh fell to the floor. Water poured down my throat, filling whatever was left of my lungs, and I drowned. The earth pulled me in, my veins bursting from air and blood and sinew.

Nothing made sense. Everything burned, and yet nothing happened.

Memories slapped into me, one after another. Walking away from Rowen. Pushing at Trace and telling him that he was nothing. That he was second best and would never be my sister's. Shoving at Alden and telling him that he was worthless. Looking into the eyes of a young widow's face as I told her that her husband's pension was forfeit.

Looking into my sister's eyes as I told her that I had taken over another company, and I would break it into parts to make more money for myself.

Every horrible thing I had ever done slammed into me, one after another, and I knew there would be no forgiveness, no time where I would ever be the hero or ever be someone worth wanting or saving.

Why were they doing this? Why were they giving me

the piece of my soul as if I deserved to live when I knew I didn't?

I had lost everything, and I had become the one person I knew I could never be.

I had become the Ash Christopher of hell, of torments, and now I was here, and I had to face what I had done. I had to face those that I had shoved off, had torn apart, had done everything but kill.

Because I was death.

And now I was life.

I fell to the ground, my body shaking as I curved into the fetal position, trying to suck in deep lungfuls of air.

The others were shouting as the magic funneled into me, the sounds like a tornado coming directly at me. And then there was silence, the vacuum being popped, and Aspen and Frank were helping Rowen to her feet. But she shoved them off and crawled to me, as Rome held Sage and Jaxton held Laurel.

I looked up at Rowen, my body shaking, and I knew.

The bond. It was there. After all this time. It was there.

Tears slid down my cheeks as Rowen wiped them away and kissed me softly. "Ash."

"I'm sorry," I whispered. "I'm so damn sorry."

For what? For everything.

I had what I wanted. My soul. My power.

And I would do anything to not feel this again because I didn't deserve it. Because I had been the man of my nightmares.

And as Rowen held me and as the others cleaned up the mess around me, I lay there and knew that no amount of forgiveness or repentance would make this better.

I was Ash. I was with a soul.

And I did not deserve forgiveness.

CHAPTER

TEN

Rowen

Guilt racked me as I pushed everyone else out of the house. Rome and Jaxton had helped me get Ash to my bed. That way he could sleep it off and try to heal. But getting everyone else out of the house had been a chore. Even pushing Laurel out had nearly killed me. But she seemed to understand that Ash couldn't be around others right now. Not because he was a danger to them, but I was afraid he would be a danger to himself.

The spell had worked.

Somehow the spell had worked.

I hadn't let myself think that it could or that it

wouldn't. I'd had to let myself not think of a single thing throughout all of this so I could focus on what needed to be done. And I could focus on not thinking about what Ash and I had done the night before.

I couldn't believe we had slept together. That, after all this time, we had so easily fallen into our bad habits. Or maybe it couldn't be a bad habit if it hadn't happened in so long.

I could still feel him inside me, the way he had held me, the way he had been far rougher than he had ever been before. And I had relished in it, needed it. It had been far more than anything I had ever thought possible, and yet it had been a mistake.

I couldn't deny that. Not when I knew sleeping with him would only complicate things.

Because I loved him.

I loved him. And I hated myself for it. Because I had known he would never be able to come back to me. Even now, as I wiped sweat from his brow as he slept, his body shaking, I didn't know if he was back.

It was hard to hope, hard to want.

Because I didn't know if he could ever love me again the way he had, not when everything had changed. Not when he wasn't that person. He had gone through so much, of his own accord, and yet not at the same time.

In that respect, I didn't know if I loved the man from before, or the man he had become. I wasn't sure I could reconcile the two, because they were not the same. This new person, with a soul, but knowing what he had done? I wasn't sure if I knew if I could love him.

That was a lie.

Because my heart sung to him.

As did the bond that had snapped back into place.

The bond that burned and ached and made me scream inside.

Because it was the same bond as before, ragged, burnt at the edges, scratched and torn.

It had gone through hell, but it had come back, just like Ash had.

Both had left me before.

I leaned forward, pushed his hair from his face. He opened his eyes quickly, and I stared into the blue pools.

"Rowen."

I pressed my lips together, played with his hair. "Ash."

"Everything hurts."

"I know. I'm sorry."

"Why are you sorry? You saved me. Because you're Rowen, and that's what you do."

I didn't hear any bitterness in his voice. Not like the Ash of coldness would have. Instead, there was only awe. As if that was what he was used to.

I wasn't sure I could put these two people together in my mind. It was as if the Ash that I had loved as a teenager had been pushed through the hell of soulless Ash and was now laying here in front of me, a completely new person, and one I couldn't figure out.

Then again, maybe the problem was Ash couldn't do the same.

"Can I get you something to eat? To drink?"

He shook his head, then sat up, groaning.

"I should get you some broth or something. You should eat and rest."

He raised a brow at me, his lips twitching. "You say that as if I've been an invalid for long. As if I have been sick for all this time. But we both know that wasn't the case." He reached out as if to touch me, then let his hand fall. I ignored the ache at the lack of touch, at the hesitancy. It was as if we were two strangers; I wasn't sure what I was supposed to say or do.

"Is everybody gone then?" Ash asked as he frowned and slid his hands through his hair.

I nodded. "You needed your rest, and I noticed that with everybody surrounding you, you tensed up even more."

He nodded tightly and ran his hands over the Ravenwood symbol on his chest. The tall redwood trees of ink on his arms and back shifted slightly, as if moving in the wind, and I wanted to reach out and trace them. I loved his anchor. The sturdiness of it, the fact that yes, they bent, were not unyielding, but did not break. In contrast, my dandelions seemed to float around and be wherever they needed to be, but they didn't have a set place to rest. In my mind, I had always thought I would be able to rest with Ash. He would be the one I would lean on when things got to be too much. That hadn't happened before, and I didn't know if I trusted myself to allow it to happen now.

"I don't need broth. I'm not hurting anymore. Other than actually feeling this thing called remorse."

I flinched. "That wasn't you."

He laughed, but it wasn't hollow like before. This time it was filled with so much pain, I wanted to reach out and hold him. But I didn't. I didn't know if that was my right, even with the bond between us. Even though I could still feel him along those jagged edges.

"I was that man, Rowen. That's the problem. That's always been the problem. Although I had no recourse to stop myself from doing what I did, nothing to hold me back other than my sister's words most times, I still did everything. I was still that man. I still stole and cheated and lied. I still pushed you away. I fought with Trace and refused to speak to him for years." Ash met my gaze, and I reached out despite myself and gripped his hand. He held on tightly as if I was his lifeline, and maybe I was. Because he had been mine before. And then I had learned to stand on my own two feet.

"Trace is gone, and the hollow part of me was the one here when I had to say goodbye. I couldn't say goodbye before the way I needed to because I wasn't here. I didn't feel the way I needed to. My sister died, and yet I felt nothing."

I shook my head. "That's a lie."

His eyes widened. "What?"

"You tried to sacrifice yourself multiple times for your sister. You said you came back to town for power, and yet you did everything you could, even fighting to get your soul back knowing it could kill you, for something. Is that power? Or is that some part of you that's always been there, screaming and hiding within."

"If I believe that, then that part of me screaming had to know it wasn't strong enough to stop the worst of it."

"But you didn't kill. You didn't force. You didn't do the things that are pure evil."

"So perhaps we can get into the philosophical discussion of does a soul make you good or does a lack of soul make you evil."

"You were evidence that lack of a soul doesn't make you evil."

"So, I suppose that with my soul now, I'm not inherently good."

I moved onto the bed, nearly straddling him so I could get close to him. He still wore his pants, no shirt, and his eyes widened at the movement. "I am not good."

"Bullshit."

I smiled despite myself. "I'm not. I get angry. I'm envious of the others. I hated you and myself that you weren't here. I hated you, Ash. Even when I loved you."

He reached out and cupped my face. "Loved? As in past tense?"

I cursed under my breath. "You sure do know how to get to the heart of the matter."

"What if *you're* the heart of the matter?"

"Ash."

"I missed you."

Tears fell, and I leaned my head against his. "I missed you so much. You were gone. Just like that, the bond broke, and I had to say goodbye. And yet I couldn't because you were standing there and then you weren't, and I didn't understand, I don't understand how magic could be so cruel to do that to us."

"I don't either. Sometimes I want to hate the magic within our veins because of what it did to us. What it did to you."

"We lost so much time, Ash."

"I hurt us so much."

"The curse did that."

"The curse was me. Isn't that the problem?"

"I can't think like that. I can't only think that it was you. I have to reconcile the fact that I've loved you forever, Ash. I know that puts me in a vulnerable position, even saying those words, but I love you."

"Rowen," he whispered.

"No. Don't say anything. Don't say that you need time to think or that it's too much of anything. Because I don't know what I'm supposed to do. We are facing the end of our days here. We need to be strong to fight Oriel. We need to fight together. And now, with your soul, you have access to the powers that you didn't before. You can be the strength of our coven, the base so we can flourish. Yet all I want to do is hold you close and pretend that the past years never happened."

"I wish I could pretend that none of it happened."

"I forgive you," I whispered, not even knowing I was saying the words until they were out. But they were true. They had to be.

His eyes widened, and he shook his head.

"How can you still love me?"

"Because I always did. Because you were mine, even if I hated the person you had become because the curse took you away from me. Not because it was you. I know it makes no sense, and I know it's confusing, but I've always loved you, Ash. That's why it hurt so much when you walked away. When the bond snapped, and it looked like you didn't even care."

"Rowen, I don't know if I could even forgive myself. Not for what I've done. Not what I did to you. Because the bond broke, and part of me couldn't care. What kind of man does that make me?"

"A man who knows that the pain is out there, but you were so strong, Ash."

"That's my line for you."

"I don't want this to be a dream. You're back, Ash. I can feel you along the bond." Something burned brighter than before, something I couldn't quite name. I wasn't sure what it was, but he was different. Yes, he had a soul, but something had changed within him, and I didn't know if it was the years past, his magic increasing, or something that we had pulled with the core itself in order to bring him back.

Something was different, but he was here. Ash was here.

So, I leaned down and kissed him.

"Ash."

He slid his hands through my hair, deepening the kiss, and my breasts pressed against his chest, his other hand going down my sides, clutching my hip.

I groaned into him, knowing that this was far different than it had been when we were younger, different than in his house the night before.

This was us now, complicated and messy, doing things in the wrong order, and yet I didn't care.

Because this was Ash. My Ash.

I kissed him again, deeper this time, and he moved me, lifting me up without a care in the world, his strength turning me on like no other. I straddled him on the bed, our clothes keeping us apart, but all I wanted to do was rock against him to bring us both to completion. My magic hummed, my anchor sliding along my arm down to my fingertips to brush along his skin. He smiled against my lips, sliding his hand over my body and through my hair again.

"I've missed this. I missed you."

I bit his lip, grinning down at him. "You're back."

"I'm so fucked up, Rowen."

"Preaching to the choir here."

"Then I guess we'll be fucked up together."

I threw my head back and laughed, and he kissed my neck, sending another groan out of me. "That's one way to describe us."

"I love you. I'm sorry I didn't say it before. But I love you. Part of me has always loved you. Even when I didn't know what love was, I loved you."

I broke then, my magic escaping slightly. The wards flared with joy as the air thrummed with my magic, and the earth rattled just slightly, Ash's magic coming to fruition. The potted plant in the corner of my room bloomed, and we looked over at it, both of us wide-eyed.

"It's been a while since we twined our magic like that."

"I think we're both stronger."

Or, at least, my magic was. I wasn't. I knew that. But I didn't want to tell him. I didn't want to worry him. Not now. Not when I had just gotten him back.

So, I kissed him and pushed all thoughts of my weakness away.

Heat seared us both, and I gasped, falling back off his lap. He groaned and then put his hand over his side, his eyes wide.

His hands fell back, and I blinked down at the dragon tattoo on his side. A stylized dragon four legs and two wings connected to its back, curled up into a ball before it began to move, stretching as if coming awake after a long sleep.

"Is that..." I paused, cleared my throat. "Is that an anchor?"

"Call Rome and Jaxton. I think we might have a problem."

ELEVEN

Ash

While part of me, okay, most of me, wanted to stay in bed with Rowen and try to get back all that we had lost, there wasn't going to be time for that. Ever.

My side scorched as if somebody had literally branded me, and I looked down at the dragon on my skin. It began to slowly walk across my stomach and then back up my ribs before going up my chest and down my arms. It moved as if unsure—unaware—of how it had gotten there, well buddy, same here.

It looked as if it was weaving through the trees, and at

any other point in my life I might have smiled, looking at the curiosity and rightness of what I was seeing, and yet, something was wrong. Something was really fucking wrong.

Because that was an anchor. For a dragon. A mythical being that did not exist. Anchors literally anchored you to the paranormal part of your life. For me, it was the trees that were of earth—my magical power. Rowen was the embodiment of air, with the dandelion seeds floating within the air. Same with water and fire. Rome had a stylized bear that crawled all over his body. The same with the hawk on Jaxton. I knew Frank had a jaguar as well. Aspen had an anchor of his own, not that we had seen it. He had mentioned it in passing, and we hadn't asked him as fae had their secrets, and we weren't about to dive into them and risk war with our friends. However, I now had a dragon on my body. There were no such things as dragon shifters, not in all the books and histories and spells I had read and seen through my life. And as a man who had searched for different kinds of magic since the moment I had left Ravenwood, I would have known.

I had hunted down grimoires and histories and other forms of magic, even going all over the world to speak with other cultures and other witches and shifters to find out what they knew of curses without disclosing too much of myself.

And yet, only the magics of old, where they discuss mythical beings that had never existed outside of stories that they passed down to their children's children's children did dragons ever exist.

How could they exist now?

"Is this because I pulled into the core of the magic? That I went to the town's full magic and re-birthed something that doesn't even exist?" Rowen asked, her voice a little manic. I had never heard her sound like that before, as if she were panicking. Well, I was panicking right along with her.

"You didn't do this," I growled out the words, pain ricocheting down my spine, and Rowen glared at me.

"You say that, and yet there is a dragon anchor on your torso, and you're in pain. I can feel it along the bond."

My mouth quirked up into a smile despite myself. "We have a bond."

She narrowed her gaze at me as she helped me out of bed. "Do you think that this is the right time for that?"

"We both know far too well that time isn't guaranteed, so maybe this is the perfect time."

"Ash."

"I feel you. You're mine. You always have been. And I'm going to spend all of my days to prove to you that I'm yours."

"Ash."

"Excuse me," Rome said from the door, clearing his throat. "Not to interrupt, but we did run here because you said it was an emergency. Something to do with an anchor? We can leave, though. If you need time to cement that bond of yours."

Jaxton cleared his throat behind Rome, laughing softly, and I grinned, looking at the two men that were my best friends—feeling something I hadn't in too long. Appreciation. Love. I loved them. As brothers. And it felt like it had been far too long since I'd had them in my life.

"I'd say you could give us some time, just to get to know one another, but…" I didn't even finish the statement before Rowen cleared her throat, and then I bent over, letting out a shocked gasp. "Okay. No time for that."

"Fuck, what is it?" Rome asked as he stalked forward, that big bear of his peeking above his collar to glare at me.

I looked at his anchor, then put my hand over mine. It was shaking as if it was scared. I cursed under my breath again. "I think we're going to have a problem."

"Dragons don't exist," Jaxton stated the obvious, and Rome growled.

"I know," Rowen gasped. "I know they don't exist. They can't. But we were playing with magic unknown. What if they existed far before Ravenwood came to be, far before even the magic that we know came to be? The core of Ravenwood is elemental. The magic that keeps this town safe and keeps our own magic steady is far older than us or even our founders. What if…" Her voice trailed off.

Rome knelt before me and put his hand on my shoulder. "We need to get you to the den."

"Just in case I shift?" I asked, not truly believing the words coming out of my mouth.

"If you do shift into a dragon, which I cannot believe these words are coming out of my mouth, you're going to need some privacy. The den will keep you safe from prying eyes, even those of fellow bears, if we keep you in the circle area. And frankly, who knows what size dragon will you be? If it's a large dragon, let's not blow-up Rowen's home."

"Let's not do that. I still can't believe this is happening." She ran her hand through her hair, then let out a breath. "Okay. Let's get you there. We'll get the coven there. And I don't know who else should be there."

"Aspen, for sure," Jaxton said, narrowing his eyes. "He's far older than any of us."

We all looked at each other and nodded, and then I bent over again in pain.

Rome practically dragged me to my car and shoved me in the backseat. I lay my head on Rowen's lap, trying to suck in air. I felt like something was squeezing my insides, twisting my bones. My skin was clammy, and I was cold and hot all at the same time. But Rome was driving like a bat out of hell as Jaxton was calling in our people.

We had more important things to deal with. Oriel, revenants, the fact that something was going on with Rowen, and the magic of this town. We had to stop worrying about me and my curses and everything going on, yet something was coming out of me, and I needed to fix it. What the hell was going on?

"We've seen things that resemble zombies, witches that come back from death, an actual phoenix—another mythical creature, mind you—and goddess knows what else, why not a dragon?" Rome asked, his voice a deep growl.

I smiled even if he couldn't see me and shook my head. "Only me," I whispered, and Rowen let out a wet laugh. "I would like a quiet life. One where we could plant flowers and pretend that the world isn't going to hell."

"A quiet life could be nice, but do we know how to deal with a quiet life?" Jaxton asked with a laugh.

"Probably not," she whispered, and I squeezed her hand before I forced myself to sit up, my body shaking.

"Let's do this."

I nearly fell out of the car as Ariel, the bear beta, came forward, her eyes wide. "He smells different."

I looked over at her and inhaled, everything almost too much. Everything was too bright, too loud. Even what I was smelling melded together, and I felt like it was all overwhelming.

"What?" Rowen asked.

"I wasn't going to mention anything, but he does smell different. And not just the fact that he now has a soul."

"Oh, I missed a few things," Ariel put in and shook her head. "But this isn't my problem. Sorry. We've got patrols ready, and we're watching. But we will also give you privacy. Just tell us what you need."

Rome began speaking more, going over what was needed, and I tried to keep up, only I felt like I was going to throw up. Instead, I knelt down and sucked in a deep breath, trying not to shake too much.

"Ash."

"I don't know what I'm doing."

"If you're going to shift, then you're going to need to lean into it."

"Okay, we'll get you through this."

A few more cars pulled up, and I saw Frank park next to Laurel and Sage, Aspen pulling in behind them. People started moving around me, but I couldn't breathe or do anything other than focus on the pain inside.

Jaxton leaned in front of me and squeezed my shoulders. "Okay, tell me what you're feeling inside, other than pain. Because I can sense that pain."

I nodded tightly. "I don't know. What am I supposed to be feeling?"

"Do you feel a bond?" Rome asked as he knelt beside Jaxton.

"With Rowen, yes."

Both men's eyes widened before they smiled softly, and Rowen cleared her throat. "Not here and now. We will deal with that later."

"Understandable. Okay, first, tell me about the anchor on your body, what do you feel?"

I closed my eyes and tried to process what I was feeling. Yes, it hurt, but I also felt fear, as if it were scared with me.

"He's scared."

"Okay, this would be his first time shifting with you."

"Is your anchor a separate entity?" I asked, confused. "I thought it was you."

"It is, and it isn't. An anchor is the symbol of your shifter half. Your shifter is you, but it's also another part of you. So eventually, what your shifter feels and what you feel within your anchor will be the same thing, but for now, you two aren't one yet. When you are, it'll all be much more symbiotic."

"I'm really fucking confused," I growled.

"Good. Because we are too. Because this is all about hawks and wolves and bears, but we don't know about dragons."

"Dragons?" Frank asked as he let out a laugh. "You young kids sure get into things these days."

"There has not been a dragon on this earth in two thousand years," Aspen said into the darkness, and we all froze before turning to the fae king.

"They're real?" Nelle asked, and I hadn't even realized that Jaxton's half-mermaid sister was standing beside her mate. She had her dark hair piled up on top of her head, her coal-rimmed eyes wide. She always went with the goth look, and it worked for her, but I couldn't focus on that too much right then.

"They were real. But they went to slumber, not extinct per se, but they moved on. To where, we don't know, but they all escaped our earth. Until apparently now. There is a sense about you."

"Ariel did say I smelled weird," I ground out.

"You smell of fire, of earth, of your magic, but a shifter witch? It'll be interesting."

"They exist, and there will exist more eventually," Rome said pointedly as he stared at Sage, who blushed. I would have to ask about that soon.

"So, dragons were real then," Laurel asked, folding her arms over her chest. "That would have been nice to know."

The fae king shrugged as he leaned into Nelle, looking far too relaxed for a man telling us dragons were real. "There are many things that were real once that should be of no concern now. But with the magic that was done to bring his soul back, and was rightly done because it was needed, things changed."

"What do I do?" I let out a breath. "I will not be a hindrance to this town or this coven. I have my soul back somehow. I'm here to help, but I need to get through this first, it seems. Damn it."

"Dragons are shifters. Follow what the shifters say. We'll be here to keep you calm."

Again, I didn't like the sound of that, but I pushed thoughts of that away, and I focused on the here and now.

"You have a bond to your anchor, pull on it, let it take

control for now. It is scared, but it knows what it needs to be, and eventually you two will become one and it will make sense. I promise you."

I looked at them and nodded before I went to all fours and let out a breath. Rowen was at my side in a minute and tugged on my pants. I raised a brow. "Really?"

"Do you really want to ruin a pair of pants by shifting into them?"

"Good point."

"And on that note, I'm about to turn and go watch the perimeter or something," Laurel said with a laugh, and Sage sighed.

"I guess I'll go with you. There are some things you shouldn't see on a friend."

Jaxton let out a rough chuckle. "Okay then, let's get you naked, then you can shift to your dragon. Things I never thought I would say to one of my best friends the day that he got his soul back from the core of the town."

That gave me a laugh, the pain easing slightly, much like I knew Jaxton was trying to do.

And so, I stretched down, went to all fours, and searched for that bond with my anchor. It seemed surprised and grateful, and then it latched on to me. My bond with Rowen pulsated, keeping me warm, and I did what I needed to. I breathed.

The dragon stretched, fire sliding along my bond and down to Rowen as she let out a soft gasp of pleasure. As if she were surprised as well.

I wasn't sure what had happened next. Everything twisted in on itself, but my bones stretched, my muscles twisted, and then everything was warm, far too warm, and bright lights nearly blinded me. And somehow, I was standing far taller above the others than I ever had before.

"Dear goddess," Rome said as he widened his eyes, nearly staggering back. Sage came to his side, slid her hand into his, and just stood there, her mouth agape.

The others were looking at me then, and I realized that I was nearly as tall as some of the smaller trees, and I looked down at my scaled self, at my four legs, and at my wings.

"Oh my god," Laurel put in. "This is, you're a fucking dragon."

"A dragon," Jaxton whispered before he started laughing. "Only you would come back and be even bigger than Rome and a fucking mystical being that could probably eat revenants in his sleep. Only fucking you, Ash."

The others joined in, but I turned, confused and a little unsteady on my feet. I had no idea what to do with these large limbs of mine and I nearly stumbled into myself, but I kept myself righted. I stretched out my wings, and noticed the dark black and red scales, and frowned. What was I supposed to do with these? Fly?

"You're beautiful."

The dragon in me nearly preened, and I leaned down, my long neck stretching as I pressed my muzzle to Rowen's side. I didn't shove at her, but she staggered a bit before she wrapped her arms around my face and grinned.

"You are gorgeous. We are going to need another spell to keep you hidden from the masses, but oh my god. You are beautiful."

"And clumsy as fuck," Frank added, laughing. "We're going to need to teach you how to walk like a dragon, and fly like one. Good thing you have a big bear, a fast jaguar, a fae king, and a hawk with wings to help you. But boy, they sure do make them fun down in Ravenwood."

I looked at the others, and then at my scales, and opened my mouth to speak. A small tendril of smoke escaped my nose, and I realized that I could not speak in this form. Laurel put her hand over her mouth as she began laughing, and then Rowen held up her hands. "Okay, a quick spell to keep this secret from the others. Just a stay hidden spell."

I looked down at my claws and then up at her. "Just the three of us for now, since I don't know if you can do magic in your dragon form. Another sentence I never thought we'd say."

I nodded, the motion awkward, as the three women began their spell.

"We call on the lady of this earth. We call on the power of who we have begun. Hide our dragon and his hearth, for he is of harm to none."

It felt as if someone had put a cool liquid over my body, and the others nodded. "We'll be able to see him since we were part of the spell, but no one else will. Meaning, I think you could possibly fly, and no one would notice you," Rowen put in. "But you're going to have to watch out for planes. Oh my god. I think I need to sit down."

I reached out with my claws and caught her as she nearly fell, and she put her hands on my scaled palms and looked up at me. "Oh my god."

I stretched before I yawned, and my body pulsated again.

I let Rowen down before I bent, twisted, and found myself naked in human form, my whole body shaking.

"That was a trip."

"It seems that you don't have enough strength or control yet to keep your dragon form for long, but you have one. Well then. It seems there's a dragon and a witch of Ravenwood, a new mated pair, and some changes. Oriel won't know what hit him."

I looked at them, and then at my mate, and held her close, even as I knelt on the ground.

I didn't know what was coming next or what would happen, but maybe, just maybe, fate had given us a helping hand. After all this time, maybe we could win.

Rowen

I sat cross-legged on the office floor in my store while Esmeralda worked up front with any passing customers. I tried to focus on within. I rarely took this time for myself, using most of my daylight hours to work on wards, tinctures, and other spells. Somebody had to make the stock for the store. We used local merchants and sold books from around the world, but the spell bags and potions that aided inherent magic required a witch. And I was the witch to do that.

I ignored the pain in my heart when I remembered that sometimes Penelope had sat by my side and helped me with spell bags. She had been wonderful at picking out the perfect herbs and cinnamon sticks and other accoutrements. She had always put herself down for whatever magic that she couldn't do, and yet I knew she was far stronger than she led on. Perhaps that strength came from who she was rather than the magic within her veins, but it still counted in my eyes. She had been able to read any small healing or home and hearth spell that I had made for her and had been able to use her small magics in order to make it work.

That was power in its own right, and I had been proud to call her my friend.

Penelope hadn't been my mother, nor had she been my aunt. I'd had both of those in my life longer than Laurel had. And Penelope had been closer to Laurel than nearly anyone in town. She had been closer to Laurel than even Sage. But together, however, I had felt as if she could have been part of our coven. Only, things hadn't worked out the way that they should, and Penelope had been taken from us in the most grotesque fashion. She had died just like my aunt. Just like my parents. Just like Laurel and Ash's parents. Sage's parents were still alive, though they weren't of magic, and either truly didn't know it existed or refused to believe it. Either way, we were our own family now. But I wasn't sure how much longer we could hold out like we were. How much longer we could remain as one and as strong as we needed to be. Not with the danger of what lurked coming for us.

The magical ward surrounding the town pulsed, and I

winced, rubbing my fist over my heart. I was trying to meditate, to focus on my power as a witch and as a woman, but the wards weren't having it. This time it didn't feel as if it were someone encroaching or trespassing. No, this was due to the wards flickering in and out, not going down completely, but having a harder time than they should to stay strong.

That was because those keeping them up weren't strong enough. Somehow, the coven and I needed to come together to weave our magic as one in order to strengthen the wards. The problem was we were trying to piece together glass shards in the dome rather than a weave.

I was truly afraid the only way to protect this town and to strengthen the wards completely was to tear them down and rebuild them.

Only, we didn't have that option. Not when Oriel and his revenants were circling the town for the core of magic. Part of me wanted to resent my elders, the ancestors who had combined their magic to protect those around them. The core had evolved into this new entity, and I wasn't sure how we would be able to fix it. Or even save it.

I focused again and thought of my inner magics, of my connections to the world. A single candle lit in front of me, and I focused on the flame, letting myself relax. First at my fingertips, then up to my wrists and elbows. I let the calming sensation move up my arms and then down my back, down my legs, to my toes. Then back up again slowly, the numbing sensation working as I let it creep up the back of my neck, over my eyelids, and down into my mouth. I breathed in through my nose, out through my mouth, and I could focus again.

The wards pulsated just slightly, a warning, not of impending doom but of lack of energy. I let out a breath and put more of myself into the wards. They flourished, and I let out a shakier breath, any energy I had gained from my meditation gone.

If I wasn't careful, I wasn't going to be strong enough.

My eyes opened as I heard the bell ring over the door in the front of the building. While I could usually ignore it, I couldn't ignore this person. I could feel him coming towards me, his magic strong, lethal. It was different than it had been before. Not because he wasn't that ice man anymore, not because he had a soul, but because there was a predator within him. A new type of predator.

Ash, and his dragon.

I leaned forward, blew out the candle, then pushed my hair away from my face as Ash walked in, a brow raised. "You look beautiful."

"I bet you say that to all the meditating witches in their shops." I laughed, trying to hide any discomfort that had come from a lackluster meditation session, and stretched my arms over my head. Ash's gaze went straight to my breasts, and I couldn't help but laugh.

"Enjoying yourself?" I asked.

"With you? Always." He knelt in front of me, cupped my face, and pressed his lips to mine. I sank into him, that sandalwood scent wrapping around me as if he were claiming me. He was smokier than before, and I couldn't help but wonder if that was the dragon, and not the man with memories and experiences that I had no part of.

He hadn't shifted since that first time, and none of us were sure he would ever do it again. A dragon shifter was unheard of, and even Aspen was tight-lipped, but I didn't think it was because he was keeping secrets from us. No, we didn't know what was happening when it came to Ash and to the dragon. Therefore, we couldn't rely on it in the face of battle. And I knew that must be hurting him, but Ash was strong. He was a witch. And he was the base of our coven. Not to the power of three, but the base that kept us steady.

At least that's what it would be if we had made it work. We weren't there yet. Magics that needed to be threaded together took time, patience, and power. We weren't ready.

Yet, Oriel seemed to be, and that worried me more and more with each passing day.

"I was going to come to see if you'd like to go for lunch. I didn't mean to interrupt you."

I smiled up and him and let him help me to my feet as I shook my head. "You didn't interrupt. I was finished."

"If you're sure." He met my gaze, staring at my face.

"I am. We could try that Italian place if you'd like."

"I think that's the same place that we've gone our entire lives." His lips formed a small smile, and it shook me. Not that I didn't want to see it, but because it felt as though I were seeing someone from my past on the face of my present. It was an odd dichotomy I wasn't sure I was ready for.

"Ravenwood is not fancy New York with a thousand restaurants that call to you. It's just home." I ignored the bitterness in my statement and had to wonder where it came from. Then again, maybe I didn't. This was the world traveler Ash. And I was the small-town girl. It didn't matter if you labeled us as witches with powers and the strength to save the world. I never left my town. And he had seen the world.

He had held it in his hands while I had stayed behind. He had gotten his degrees, multiple bachelor's and a couple of master's degrees, because he was so brilliant and soaked up knowledge. I had finished my degree online because the town had tied me to it. I couldn't stay away because, if I left, the wards would fail. I had a shoddy business degree with low scores because I couldn't focus and put everything into it. I hadn't even left the country. And Ash owned homes in multiple places around the world.

"What is that look for?"

Ash's voice pulled me out of my thoughts, and I shook my head, shame creeping up my spine. "I'm feeling sorry for myself. Something I would rather not do."

"Talk to me, Rowen. I thought I was the one that was supposed to feel sorry for myself."

My lips twitched into a smile, just like he intended. "I was thinking that you've done so much more than I have. Other than magic, I suppose. Our lives are so different, it's odd to think that fate would bring us together."

Ash scowled. "If you take away the magic, then we aren't who we are. And we're not together because of the magic. You know that. Or at least you knew we weren't before. I feel like I'm a completely new person, and we're finding this fresh path that we need to go down, but that's fine. We can make it work. But, Rowen, never think less of yourself because of what you had to sacrifice in order to protect your family, this town, and the strangers in it. You have done everything in your power to save the fucking world. Don't think of yourself anything less."

"Well, when you put it like that," I teased, even though there was a kernel of that doubt there. It would fester if I didn't take care of it, but there were far more important things to worry about other than my own emotional well-being. Or at least my jealousy when it came to it.

"Let's get us something to eat. I'll ask Esmeralda if she'd like us to bring her something."

I blinked. "You know her name? I didn't realize you know that."

Ash looked away a bit, and then I realized I shouldn't have said anything. "I knew it before. Because I tried my best to know everyone around me so I could use them in some way if needed. But I knew. I didn't use her name before because the part of me that cared wasn't there. But

I knew. And I'm going to do better about making amends for the asshole that I was."

"If I can't think down on myself for the decisions I've been forced to make, you can't either."

Ash was silent for so long that I was afraid I'd once again said something wrong. Odd, it used to be Ash that always did so, but now it was me who couldn't keep up. "I suppose for each of us, it's easier said than done."

I opened my mouth to say something, but the wards flared, and this time it wasn't a normal function. No, this was something far worse. "Revenants, Behind us."

Ash's eyes glowed, and I wondered for a moment if it was his magic, but no, that was the dragon. Something else to get used to. "Can you call the others through the coven?"

My heart twisted and I shook my head. "It didn't work last time."

"Because Oriel was holding it back. Keep trying, and I will call Rome. We will get this done."

I liked the sound of his optimism, while I hoped that it wasn't misplaced. Not when I didn't feel steady on my feet, and Ash hadn't been in a battle with his new soul and his connection to his powers. We weren't ready. Despite a lifetime of preparing, we weren't ready. And it shamed me.

After calling Esmeralda to stay safe and lock it down, I ran out the back and found myself staring at revenant after revenant behind the alley that connected our street to the forest. A small creek that fed into the larger river was burbling as if someone was sending magic into it, but it didn't feel like water. No, it felt like air.

The hairs on the back of my neck stood on end. "Oriel. He's here. But not. He's sending his revenants, and he's doing something with the creek, but I don't know what."

"It feels like when I'm trying to mold the water, but I fail at it," Sage said as she came forward.

I frowned and looked at my friend as she ran towards us. "You're right, but more so, it's as if I were to use my air magic and slice underneath the water itself, but I don't have you with your power to guide it."

Sage nodded as she came to my side and rolled her shoulders back. "Then we fight. Because he doesn't have a water witch with him now and, from what we can see, he's alone. But we aren't."

"He's not completely alone," Laurel added, as she ran towards us, sword in hand, with Jaxton flying overhead.

"He's still got that fire bitch."

"Then we fight."

Ash rolled his shoulders back. "I don't think I'm able to shift to my dragon."

"We don't know how to fight in that form. It wouldn't be good," Rome grumbled as he looked up at Jaxton.

Laurel let out a breath. "Jaxton's going to stay in that form. He's had a long day of shifting thanks to wing issues." I met her gaze. She shook her head. "Nothing bad. Just normal wing things, but he's exhausted. So, he's going to stay in that form."

Worry etched through me, but I ignored it because we needed to be stronger. "We push through, and we try to keep the revenants at bay before we fight."

"I'll watch you do what you need to do, but take out any stragglers," Rome growled, his claws out. He was in human form, but even so, with the claws and fangs, he could rip out the throat of any revenant that came near. I knew, however, with the dozens or so slowly crawling towards us, it wasn't going to be enough unless we corralled them.

I knew with communication lines that we had in place that the other shifters and Aspen, and even some of the witches and humans, were keeping the town safe in their sections, but we were the ones that were charged with fighting on the front lines. This was our job. I had to trust in the other parts of the town to keep themselves safe. Or alert us if there were larger issues.

"Which spell?" Laurel asked as she took my hand. Ash took the other, as Sage took his.

"The banishment spell."

Laurel nodded, and I let my magic reach through me, and we spoke.

"Banish the evil and those who wish harm. Give us courage to pick up our arms. Sisters, brothers, ancestors, friends, our strength is unrivaled and without end. Lords and Ladies, spirit guides, too, guide us and protect us in all we must do. Today is our day, together we rise, victory is ours from earth to skies!"

Only, it didn't work. I knew the moment we said the

words that it wasn't enough. The wards fluctuated at the exact instant that we finished speaking, and they stripped my magic, just for a bare instant, but I screamed, blood pouring down my nose as I fell to my knees. Sage and Laurel looked at me for a moment, but then they couldn't help because they needed to fight what was in front of us as the revenants came closer, going through the water as if nothing was holding them back. And that's what Oriel was doing. He was using the air magic to guide the revenants towards us without having to be there.

Laurel and Jaxton fought one side of the enemy, her sword catching fire as she sliced through a revenant. Jaxton swooped down, his talons clawing out the eyes of the nearest corpse, and then deeper, leaving gouges as the revenant fell and Laurel used her fire to burn it to ash. Sage mumbled spells underneath her breath, using the water from the creek against Oriel's own magic to push at the revenants. At the same time, Rome took those coming closer to her and killed them instantly. I finally noticed that Sage also had a bat in her hand and used the strength that she had been given through hours and hours of training with Rome to smash the head of one revenant and then another.

They were working alongside their mates, fighting, and winning. And yet, I hadn't been able to use my magic and my strength to stop the revenants in their tracks in the first place.

This was my family, the coven's family. And it wasn't enough.

Ash turned me towards him and wiped the blood from my nose. "Fuck."

That was it. There wasn't much else to say.

He knew what was happening, at least part of it, and we weren't strong enough right then. And I hated myself. I tried to fight, but I couldn't stand on my two feet. Ash held me up, smoke drifting out of his nose as his dragon came forth, but he didn't shift. He couldn't. And I couldn't fight.

Instead, I let the others take out the revenants. Frank came forward and helped in his jaguar form, and Aspen and Nelle came to clean up the mess.

I leaned on the ground, my body shaking as magic faded from me before rushing back in, but I didn't reach for the core. I didn't search for Oriel. I just tried to breathe.

I tried to tell myself I wasn't dying. Only, I knew if I spoke those words aloud, they would be a lie.

CHAPTER
THIRTEEN

Ash

The following morning, I stood on Rowen's porch wondering what I should do. Nervousness ebbed inside me alongside the dragon I couldn't quite name as it grumbled slightly before going to sleep. It was odd to think that, after so many years, I was more like Rome and Jaxton than before. I was a shifter. One who didn't know how to control it and didn't know if it would ever come back, but I was a shifter.

And I had no idea what that meant.

However, today was not about me, my soul, or my dragon. No, it was about the woman who made me want to tear my hair out, the one that I wanted to fall on my knees before as I begged for forgiveness.

And one I've wanted to yell at because she wasn't taking care of herself. Well, if she wasn't going to do it, then I was going to do it for her. I had been gone for too long, but now I was back. So, I would take care of her. Even if she resented me for it.

The door opened, and Rowen stood there in a short breezy dress, the copper fabric silky along her thighs. It had long bell sleeves and looked more like a house dress that she might pair with something fancier if we ever went out. Not that we did that. There was no time for anything along those lines these days.

"Why are you staring at me?" She looked down at her bare feet and legs and shrugged. "I thought I would look cute today because I'm not feeling great, but instead I just look weird."

I reached forward, gripped the back of her head, and pulled her in for a kiss. She moaned into me, and I bit her lip, smiling as she pinched my side. "You look sexy as fuck. I was just thinking I hadn't seen you in a short dress like this in years."

"I tend to wear long flowing skirts, but I wanted to wear this one."

She pulled me into the house, and I closed the door behind me. She looked down at herself, pulled at the ends of her dress. "I rarely get to wear cute clothes like this these days. Nowhere to wear it. Plus, I don't like to show off this much skin."

The collar of her dress went up to her neck, the lace playing peek-a-boo. The only skin she showed was far more thigh than I knew she liked to bear, and my mouth watered.

"I like it."

"And I suppose that's all that matters." She winked, and it felt as if we were both playing a game where we figured out who we were *now*. "Honestly though, I've never worn it, I bought it on a whim, so I thought I would wear it at home while I'm looking at my grimoires."

Interest piqued, I looked behind her. "What are you studying?"

"I'm just looking for ways to strengthen the wards and to stop Oriel somehow. He has more power than us because he can access the dark magics. It pisses me off, frankly."

"It's a cheat." My dragon grumbled along with me.

"A cheat that is so evil that it makes me want to throw up."

I sighed and leaned forward, inhaling that sweet and spicy scent of hers. "You don't have to always do it on your own."

"You say that, and yet I feel like I'm two steps behind. He has so much magic. And we can't pull on it."

"We're stronger together."

She looked at me then, her eyes warm. "It's like you're a different person. And yet the same. Not just the same as you were before, but the same person you were last week."

I shrugged and walked past her to her workroom where she had her books laid out, notes strewn about, dried flowers and herbs hanging around the fogged windows of her greenhouse. I tried to get my thoughts together since I wasn't sure what I felt to begin with. "I still am that person. All three. Because I can't take away the memories or the actions. I'm still the man who made those choices. Still the man who broke something inside. I can't change that."

"And maybe you shouldn't. Because if we push it underneath the rug, are we any better than Oriel?"

I turned to her then, a wry smile playing on my face. "No, we're not any better. But I suppose that's the problem, isn't it?"

She let out a sigh and leaned forward, brushing her fingers along my collar. My magic pulsed, aching for her like always. "I guess it's hard to reconcile the two different parts."

"Or maybe more than two," I said after a moment. "Either way, we can't go back. I know that. So, that means I'm going to need you to tell me what the fuck is going on, Rowen." My voice went cold. As cold as it had been before I had regained my soul.

"What do you mean?" she said.

I scowled. "Don't lie to me. Not now. Not ever. Tell me."

"It's fine."

"Something's wrong. You keep passing out. I know the magic is too much. But what exactly is going on? No more platitudes, no more telling me that you're going to make it through and it's just that you're tired or that the wards are just a little too much that day. Because it's every day, and it's getting worse."

"I don't want to talk about it," she whispered.

I leaned forward, cupped her face. "No. We don't get to do that. Not now. Not ever."

"What if I have to do that to survive?"

My heart twisted and I let out a calming breath so I wouldn't yell. "Then we're going to have a problem. Because I need you to always be able to come to me." I paused, knowing I needed to say what was coming next. "Are the wards killing you?"

She pressed her lips together before her face fell. "Yes. Every time the wards break, every time a revenant gets through, or we are attacked, or I have to use my magic in a way that I hadn't before, it's weakening me. I thought maybe it just meant that the wards would break, and we'd have to rebuild them, but no, I think it's different now. I think I'm in trouble."

I had known. *I had known this.* There was no other way. I had known that it was hurting her, that something was terribly wrong. But I had wanted her to deny it. Even though we had spoken of it weakening her, I had wanted her to deny it.

"Then untether yourself. Don't let yourself be part of this. Walk away. We'll protect the town another way. You don't have to do this."

She smiled softly. "Can I? Can I walk away just like that? From everything? Because you know I can't, you know that doing so would break me."

"*You're breaking me.*"

I hadn't meant to say the words aloud.

"We have honor. We know that. I can't let go of the wards and let the innocent die because of me."

"And I can't let you die."

"I don't think we're going to have a choice. Unless we break Oriel and we have more time or find something in one of these grimoires to strengthen the wards, I can't untether myself. And it has nothing to do with my wants." She met my gaze. "I can't do it," she whispered, and my heart shattered.

"Rowen."

"Just kiss me." She shook her head. "We know what's coming is going to be terrible. That even though we have the strength of the coven, that there's something wrong because of Oriel. We know all this. It's not news. You know this. But you're just now back. You're finally back to me. And I can't breathe. So just hold me. Kiss me. Make love to me. And just let me forget."

I had no words. There was nothing for me to say to

make this any better. Not when I knew if I tried to do something, it could make matters worse, not when I wasn't thinking clearly. So, I would do what she asked. And I would let her forget. As long as I could find a way to forget with her.

I gently kissed her, sliding my hands through her hair as she grinned into me, though I knew that smile wasn't full and probably forced, because the woman that I loved was dying.

Just like I had been before, she had sacrificed everything for me.

I would protect her, and then maybe, just maybe, she would let me do more.

I pushed her hair back from her face, kissing her gently, then a bit harder. I tugged her back to the couch, and she grinned, laughing as she fell onto me. She sat sideways on my lap, her legs crossed at the ankles on the couch as I planted my feet on the ground. Then I slid my hands up her thighs, the pads of my fingers gently caressing her bare skin. She shivered as I put my other hund on the small of her back and she arched for me. I nuzzled her breasts through her dress and bit down lightly over her nipple. My eyes widened when I realized she was bare underneath, and she licked her lips.

"I liked the feel of silk and lace on my skin."

I groaned, her ass over my covered cock, and I swallowed hard. "I'm going to come in my pants like a teenager."

"You better not. Because I want you inside me."

"Then I suppose I'll have to do better."

I gently cupped her bare ass underneath the dress, marveling at the fact that while she didn't wear a bra, she also didn't wear underwear. We were slow, taking our time, as I gently spread her ass cheeks, playing with her, before sliding my hands between her folds, probing her wet entrance. She shivered, spreading her legs for me, and I removed my hands, pressing her thighs back together.

"No. I'm in charge today."

"Ash."

"You're mine, Rowen. Let me take care of you."

I continued to kiss her, gently rubbing along her skin, before I pulled up her dress slightly, exposing her to me.

She was bent over my lap, her legs crossed at her knees as she laid over me. Her head was slightly above mine, so her breasts were at my mouth, and I kissed her through the dress again, this time twisting her slightly so her core was over my lap, her ass in the air. I gently played with her then before pushing up her dress completely, both of us groaning as she moved over my cock. We couldn't move her dress completely over her head at this angle, so I whispered under my breath, and her dress disappeared.

She threw her head back and laughed. "Ash."

"I want you like this, at this angle, when I pleasure you. I'll use my magic the way that I have to."

She groaned again as I latched onto her nipple,

sucking and tugging as she writhed over my lap. I had one hand behind her back, keeping her in place as I sucked on her nipples, and with her arched over me, her ass in the air over my lap, I gently spread her before playing with her folds. She was wet, glistening, slick over my fingers, and when I gently probed her, she shivered. She reached around, arching her breasts more into my mouth as she gripped my cock through my pants. She squeezed and I groaned, spearing her with two fingers. I gently played with her, sliding over her clit, twisting my fingers to find her G-spot. She was wet and slick, and as I went faster, the sounds we were both making, grunts and heavy breaths, I slammed into her, two fingers, then three, her ass shaking in the air as I fucked her with my fingers. She squeezed my cock, and I sucked on her nipples harder, biting, leaving bruises. And when she came, arching over my body, I slid my fingers out of her, then slapped her ass. I rubbed the sting over her flesh, then smacked her again, then again, again. Her skin was a rosy hue and her eyes darkened, the magic around us floating in the air as we twined together.

I kissed her again, then shoved her up and face down on the couch. She groaned at me, smiling, and I undid my belt, shoved my pants down, and slammed into her in one thrust. I gripped her hips as she pushed back into me, and I fucked her hard, no more slowness, no more sweetness. This was just the two of us, needing. She snapped her fingers, muttering under her breath with another spell, and my clothes disappeared. I grinned, pulled out of her, and then twisted her around to lift her up. I held her thighs as I slammed her over my cock, with me kneeling one knee on the couch, my other foot planted on the ground, and I pulled her up over my cock and then back down again. Her breasts bounced as we made love, going harder and harder. And when I shook, both of us nearing our pleasure, I pulled out of her again, laid her on the couch, and spread her thighs. I sucked on her cunt, licking and probing, twisting my lips around her clit. When she came again, I kept going, sucking out her orgasm, and then I gently slid my fingers lower, below her pussy, using her wetness to prepare her. She groaned, spreading her legs more, and I gently probed her ass and grinned.

"Are you ready?"

"Always. For you. Always."

I looked around the workshop, was thankful to see a bottle floating towards us, and I shook my head.

"Of course, I have some. You know me. All natural."

I grinned, leaned down to kiss her again, and then used her natural lubricant to wet her and my cock. And when I pushed inside, both of us groaned, and the magic sparkled around us, little shots of light humming in the air. We were gentle, both of us taking our time as I gently slid my thumb over her clit, keeping her steady, and then I was deep inside, both of us groaning at the intensity. I moved slowly, knowing I wasn't going to last very long, and then she began to move quicker, and I caught up to her, and when she came again, her body squeezing me, I came with her, filling her up, both of us shaking with need.

I held her close, telling myself that this wasn't the last time. It hadn't been the last time when I thought I had been the one dying. And it wouldn't be the last time now.

Afterward, we cleaned ourselves up and held each other naked on the couch, both of us just catching our breaths.

"We'll find a spell."

"I think I know what I need to do." There was a sureness in her tone that caught my attention.

I looked down at her and squeezed her hip. "What do you need me for?"

"I think I need to speak with the ancestors. To the founders. We need to find out how to protect the core of the town."

"If we do that, we need to figure out how to cut you off from the wards. Because when the wards fall, and we both know that's a possibility, I refuse to let you go."

She cupped my face and kissed me softly. "We might not have a choice."

"Then I will fight to the end of the world to make the choice for us."

I crushed her to me as the tears fell down her cheeks. Rowen never cried, and yet with each passing day, she did more and more.

For that alone, I would tear Oriel's heart out.

I did not care that he was blood. That he was Ravenwood.

He was a traitor, an abomination.

I protected what was mine.

No matter the cost.

CHAPTER
FOURTEEN

Rowen

Between work, battles, preparation, and healing, I felt as if we hadn't had time as our new family in weeks. Or perhaps we never had. Not since everything had shifted. But tonight, we were going to breathe, eat, and just be for a little bit.

"Everything smells wonderful," Sage stated as she walked into my kitchen. I looked over at the little witch and smiled.

"I hope it smells wonderful. We've been cooking for hours."

"I've always loved using fresh herbs and things in my bread, but I never really had a chance to have an herb garden right outside my home. I enjoy being able to pick certain things, to be able to use the freshest ingredients available."

"Are you and Rome fixing up the garden then? I know he had a decent one outside his home in the den, but it's probably not up to a witch's standard." I winked as I said it, and she rolled her eyes.

"Sometimes, I feel like Rome is a better gardener than even I am. He just never had the time to get into it."

"So, the two of you are making it your own?"

"We are. We're also still planning a larger mating ceremony, one where his parents can come down and stay, and we can just be. I know we had a smaller ceremony already, and we're mates, and there's no taking that back, but we want to celebrate. To bring the pack closer together. But we're waiting."

I nodded tightly. "To take care of Oriel first."

Sage winced. "I'm sorry. I know we were trying to make tonight a little less business and a little more family-oriented, and here I am, bringing him up."

"It's not your fault. We need to be able to talk about him fully and perhaps make plans, but we can also eat good food and plan your mating ceremony."

"Did someone say mating?" Laurel asked as she walked in, a smile on her face. She wrapped her arms around Sage's waist and kissed Sage on the temple. "We're going to have our joint one, right?"

They grinned at each other, and my heart clenched a little, even though I was so happy for my friends.

Sage smiled softly. "That's the plan. Although I always think that you're going to have vastly different ideas on mating ceremonies than I will."

"Oh honey, it's not going to be you and me. We can find the perfect witchy alternative and center for the two of us. No, it's going to be the boys that are the issue."

I laughed, shaking my head as I stirred the potatoes. "She's right. Bears and hawks have a vastly different concept of a mating ceremony."

"That's not ominous at all. Though I guess we probably should have talked about this a bit more before now."

"When would we have had time?" Laurel asked, shaking her head. "It feels like you've been here for years, but you haven't."

"No, no time at all has passed, and yet everything has changed."

The girls looked at me then, and I smiled. "You're right. Everything has changed."

"Do you want to talk about it?" Sage asked as she gripped my hand. I squeezed her hand back, and I shook my head.

"Not right now. Maybe as a group over dinner, but Ash and I do have a few things to discuss first."

"I want to be happy for you," Laurel whispered. "But it's hard to be optimistic when it doesn't even feel real."

"My thoughts exactly. Now, go put the green beans on

the table."

Laurel made a face. "Why do I always have to deal with the vegetables?"

"Because I love watching your face. I also made caramelized brussels sprouts, so you're going to have to get over that too."

Laurel pretended to gag, but I shook my head. "There is bacon in them, your favorite. So don't even."

"Did someone say bacon?" she asked as she grabbed both the green beans and the brussels sprouts from the island and headed towards the dining room.

Sage came to my side. "What can I do?"

"I just need to scoop up the potatoes, as well as the cornbread stuffing."

My sister witch smiled. "I already placed the two types of bread on the table."

"And you made the crusty toasted bread for our charcuterie board earlier, and I feel like I'm eating way too many carbs." I put my hand over my stomach, and Sage rolled her eyes.

"You look amazing, and we both know that you need the extra calories. So don't even pretend that you're eating too much."

She met my gaze, and I nodded tightly. "You're right. However, let's eat and enjoy ourselves."

"I'm here to help with the meat," Ash put in, and Sage rolled her eyes as I let out a laugh.

"Really?"

My mate winked. "What? I can't help it. I'm really good with meat."

"And on that note, I am running away." Sage picked up the breads and just shook her head.

"Okay, that's enough about your meat. Help me with the roast and the chicken."

"There's only six of us. Are you feeding an army?" He asked as he leaned in and pressed his lips to the side of my mouth. Sage let out a little sigh as she walked out of the kitchen, her hands full.

I leaned back, meeting his gaze. "So, we're just doing this. Not talking, just doing it."

"By doing it, you mean figuring out who we are together again? You're right. We're doing that. Because we're mates, I can feel you in my soul. I can feel your anchor wrapping its dandelion fluff around the cord between us and the earth within me, pulling it in. We've always been one. It's just been muted. The consequences of which are something we're going to need to unravel at one point, but you're it for me, Rowen. You always have been."

"Just like that."

His gaze clouded, and I swallowed hard, knowing I was pushing the issue because I was scared, so scared that he was going to lose his soul again, or I was going to lose him. Instead, he cupped my face, kissed me softly. "Just like that. We'll figure it out. I'm not going to hide our bond from the others. They already know anyway. They can feel the magic. Feel us. So, we're going to eat, we're going to live in the moment, and then we're going to take the next steps to protect this town. All the while, I'm going to find a way to redeem all the shit that I've done in the past few years."

"Ash," I began, but he shook his head.

"It's all true. I need to fix the mistakes, and I will. So, for now, it's you and me."

"Okay. We'll figure it out."

He kissed me again, and I had to wonder how I was here, how this had happened. Only, I knew there was no real going back. No fixing things. Fates didn't allow for time like that.

"What's taking so long?" Rome asked as he clapped his hands. "I'm hungry, and I need meat. Although, according to Sage, somebody's already talking about meat a little too freely in front of my mate." He scowled as he said it, and I rolled my eyes.

"Okay, enough talking about your meats. Let's eat."

The others helped me take everything else out of the kitchen and into the dining room. I sat next to Ash, and Laurel beamed at us, even though there was worry in her gaze.

Ash was back. Our Ash was back.

Finally.

I just had to hope that this wasn't going to be the end. That I wasn't going to have him back and then so quickly leave him because of the powers out of our control.

"So, you're telling me that you're far more attached to the core of the town than we thought?" Laurel asked after dinner. We sat in the living room, dishes washed, bellies full, and Ash and I finally told the others what was going on with me. They had known, of course, just not the extent of it. They'd always known that if I left Ravenwood for too long, the wards pulled on me, and that they would fade. There had been no hiding that, and I had been open about it. Only we had all incorrectly surmised that once the coven was whole, I wouldn't be the sole person holding the wards. And while that was partially true, it was not all of it. Because there needed to be more. Something was missing, and I had to wonder what it was.

"I wish there was a way we could just go back and ask the founders what they did." I looked up at Sage's words and frowned.

"What?"

"There's something that we're missing, something that hasn't been passed along in our books or down family lines. Why is your soul so entwined with the wards and the core when you didn't even do that? Yes, you used your blood to create a spell and to strengthen it, but we are all of blood. We have all shed that blood. We should be part of it, too. There is something else we're missing. And I wish we could just ask them."

I met Ash's gaze, he nodded tightly.

"Sometimes it takes a new witch to think of old magic," he murmured, and Sage frowned between us.

"What are you talking about? What did I say?"

"There's a way. A way we could ask."

Sage's eyes widened. "You're not going to turn dark, are you? Not going to turn to a necromancer and bring them back? Because that's not what I meant. At all. Forget I said anything."

Rome wrapped his arms around his mate and kissed the top of her head. "I'm going to hope that's not what they mean. No, I think we're missing something here."

"Care to enlighten us?" Jaxton asked, and Laurel shrugged.

"Actually, I don't know. You'd think I would, considering I'm her oldest friend."

I winced. "It was something in a book passed down through my family from the founders. Something that Ash and I had read once." I blushed, thinking about exactly what we had not been wearing when we had read about it, and Ash chuckled.

"I know what you're thinking about," he mumbled, and Laurel let out a gagging sound.

"Okay, let's focus."

"We can do a spell right here, to call to the ancestors, to speak to them. It is a provision that they left when they built the core. I've never done it because it takes a full coven, and we haven't had it until now." I looked around at my friends, at their mates, and I swallowed hard. "But we should. We should call forth the ancestors."

"Tonight," Sage said with a nod, and I swallowed.

"Although I would think that idea would be a little rash and a little more Laurel's speed," I began, and Laurel flipped me off. "Either way, you're right. We should do this."

"Okay then. We'll do it right now. Will this alert Oriel?" Rome asked as he leaned forward, his forearms on his knees.

I shook my head. "We changed the wards of my home, which are far easier to do because they were newer and mine, not the town's. So, he won't be able to sense what we're doing, but we have feasted broken bread, and we are a family and a coven tonight. With the moon at it's phase, this is the best time."

"With no preparations? Is that possible?" Jaxton asked, and I nodded tightly.

"Now we can do it. You and Rome will be part of it though, as coven, not just protectors."

Rome's brows rose. "We're not witches."

"But you carry the magic along the bonds, and it will strengthen the coven." I let out a shaky breath. "I think that's what has been missing. A full coven. Of mates and of power." I met Ash's gaze. "I wouldn't let myself see it, for obvious reasons."

Ash cupped my face, rubbed his thumb along my cheekbone. "We're seeing it now. Let's do this."

I had all the ingredients in my workshop. We salted the circle, added our herbs, and we stood as six, Ash on one side, Rome on my other. Laurel stood by her brother, while Sage stood by her mate. We were power, and we were strength, and it was time to do something I had long since forgotten.

"In our hopes and in our hearts, we call forth those who are in our pasts, our futures, and of our blood. We call forth the protection of our pasts and bring forth the ancestors we know who are our pasts."

Power radiated through us as a purple mist mixed with blue and red seeped out of Laurel's, Sage's, and my skin. The men had more of a silver mist, combining together in a knot in the middle, while the other colors wrapped around the cord the silver made. It was of strength and of base that we were able to magic ourselves within.

I closed my eyes for a moment, letting the warmth of magic and power tingle over my skin, the spell done far easier than I had ever thought possible. But it was the strength of the group rather than the strength of one that even made it possible.

A cool hand caressed my cheek, and I opened my eyes. Standing before me was a woman that looked so much like my reflection. I nearly gasped and took a step back. But I didn't, knowing if I broke the circle now, the ancestors would be gone.

Instead, I looked at the first Ravenwood as she smiled at me. She wore a long flowing white dress, her hair billowing in the wind of her own magic.

"Rowen. It is so good to see you. In the flesh, as it were."

The others gasped, and I saw six spirits within the circle. It was not just my ancestor, but a male Christopher of earth, a female Christopher of fire, a Prince witch of water that looked so much like Penelope I nearly gasped. Then there was a giant of a bear—an alpha—and a slender yet strong and wiry hawk. They were the founders, not just of witches. The parts that we had been missing over time. Ideas began to tingle in my mind, and I set them aside for now.

"You came. Blessed be."

"Blessed be," the Ravenwood whispered. "We are all here, but I am the voice for now. For you are the leader, therefore, heir to heir, I am here for you."

I nodded as the others turned, and the spirits within our circle met each of our gazes, nodding and bowing in front of us.

The power tingled over my skin, but it wasn't too much. It was just our strength.

"Thank you for coming. We needed to speak to you about the core magic, the wards, and what is happening."

The Ravenwood smiled. "We know what is happening. We have been watching, though unable to do anything but watch and hope. You, as a coven of six, are stronger than you'll ever know."

My eyes widened. "Of six?"

The Ravenwood smiled. "Daughter of mine, the coven

has been of a witch, but not only. There is magic within the anchor, within the alphas. Rely on the bonds."

"You're saying that Jaxton and Rome are coven?"

"They are the coven that surrounds the coven of four. Although, to defeat this darkness, you may need more. There are ways to do that, ways to unlock the power within that have been unreachable until this moment. Search and seek, and you shall find."

I set that thought aside, knowing it would be important later. The others were listening, letting me speak, and I knew we would talk about all of this soon, but I needed to ask more questions.

"The core of the town, is there a way to protect it? Or perhaps infuse it into the earth itself, so it's not a beacon for Oriel and the ilk of him?"

The Ravenwood shook her head. "There is no longer a time for the latter, I'm afraid. The only time that would have worked was long before you were born. In creating the core to protect the town and the earth itself against necromancers, we created a being that indeed encapsulated what the darkness is. It was not of our own making, and it was a side effect that we could not foresee. You are connected to the core irrevocably because of the solidarity you were forced to maintain. Because of the outside forces, the curses and spells that kept the others away, the core pushed itself inside of your soul in order to protect you and the town."

I nodded tightly, tears falling as the others stared at

me. "I know," I whispered.

The others gasped as they realized what had happened. Exactly what I had been trying to ignore.

"If the core goes to Oriel, your magic and your soul will go with him. You must protect yourself and the core at all costs."

Power shifted, and I knew the spell was waning. There was only so much time left with the ancestors to get the answers we needed.

"How do we protect the town?"

"You must rebuild. But before you do that, some may fall. Rely on your soul, on your memory, and those around you. Rely on who could be, rather than who is no longer. The other is strong, but together you can be stronger. Find that strength. No matter the cost."

"How do we do that?" I asked, needing answers and knowing she could give no concrete ones. The Ravenwood smiled softly, then cupped my face again with her cool touch.

"You know the answers. You will find them. Be well, daughter of mine. We watch, we wait, and we hope. For hope is all that is left for some. But you are stronger. Remember that, Ravenwood. Remember that, daughters and sons of mine."

And then they were gone. I swallowed hard, looking at the others, and wondering exactly how the hell we were supposed to protect the town when it seemed we could barely protect ourselves.

CHAPTER

FIFTEEN

Ash

"I still cannot believe we spoke to our ancestors yesterday," Jaxton said with a sigh as he leaned back against the chair, beer in his hand. He played with the edge of the label while I sat on the other side of him, Rome standing in front of us, leaning against the porch railing.

"It truly doesn't seem real, and yet, I feel like maybe we should've done it long before now." I shrugged after I said it, taking a long draw from my beer. Rome let out a slight growl before sipping his as well.

The bear alpha tilted his head. "Maybe it wasn't the right time."

I looked at him then, a smile playing on my lips. "Now, who sounds like the witchy seer."

He flipped me off while Jaxton laughed. "Things sure have changed recently."

"Do you mean the end of the world, or the fact that I'm back in whatever capacity that I am?"

Jaxton just shrugged. "It's good to have you back, man. Soul and all."

I looked between them and smiled, hoping it reached my eyes. "I'm going to always hate part of myself for what happened. For the choices I made. Or perhaps maybe the choices I had to make."

"It's not all your fault—" Jaxton began.

I shook my head, cutting him off. "That's the whole idea of if a soul makes you a better person. Perhaps we realize that wasn't the case. Because I made terrible decisions when I thought no one was looking."

Rome frowned. "You didn't make the worst decisions out there. Yes, you hurt people. But you didn't cross most lines. And you're back now."

I once again played with the label on my bottle. "And how does one atone for the sins of oneself when I don't even feel like I am that person any longer."

"If we're going to talk philosophy, I'm going to need something stronger than a honey beer," Rome added with a laugh.

"Is there honey whiskey then?" I asked, needing a

moment to just *be* after the hell we'd been through recently.

Rome beamed, his bear in his eyes. "Oh yes. I've got honey whiskey."

Soon we were taking shots of sweet liquor, laughing, and gorging ourselves on cheese and crackers. Yes, even honey Gouda and honey goat cheese. There was probably something seriously wrong with us with the amount of honey we were ingesting, but I didn't care. I would turn into a bear if I wasn't careful.

"How much honey does one need to turn into a bear?" Jaxton asked, his voice a little slurred. I didn't know how much we had drunk by then, but it was enough that I was a little worried we'd end up sleeping out on Rome's porch.

"Hey, you'd be so lucky to be a bear."

I couldn't help it, I laughed. "I was just thinking that I have enough honey in me to shift into one."

"You said it out loud, dumbass," Rome laughed.

I winced. "I feel like without a soul, I could hold my liquor better. Does a soul reduce your tolerance?" I asked, leaning back against the chair again.

Rome snorted. "This shit is made by bears and for bears. You've probably had twice the amount of liquor your little witch self could handle."

I snorted. "Excuse me. I am a dragon. I do believe dragon beats bear in the wars of size."

"Hey, let's not talk about how size matters because I could take you both down with my talons," Jaxton said, his chin raised as he set down his beer. "I could probably use some water first."

Rome laughed out a growl and then poured water from the pitcher I hadn't realized he had brought out.

"Seriously though, I'm a dragon. Shouldn't I have a better tolerance?"

"Eventually, when you learn to merge with your dragon a bit more. You've only shifted once. It'll take time."

I looked down at my arms, only saw the witch anchors, not my dragon, so I did the only thing I could. I pulled off my shirt to find the damn thing. Both guys whistled, and I flipped them off before I saw the sleeping dragon on my stomach. I tapped him, frowning. "Hey. Am I supposed to shift again? Or is this just something we did just once? What are we doing?"

"Your anchor doesn't actually talk back," Rome mock whispered. "This isn't like that one movie. It's not an extra soul. It's just the mark of who you are."

The dragon opened its eyes at my words, huffed out a little puff of smoke that looked like dark ink across my body before it stretched long and moved around. I shivered at the sensation before it landed on my shoulder, resting its head along my neck.

"That's fucking cool," I muttered, and Jaxton grinned.

"Well, ask your dragon if it wants to come out and play." He paused. "I did not mean your dick. I meant the actual dragon. I need to stop drinking bear whiskey if I'm going to be able to shift. Or hell, to ever use my dick again. Can you get whiskey dick from honey whiskey?" he asked, laughing.

"And that's enough alcohol for the hawk," Rome said on a laugh, taking away the other man's whiskey. "Water for you."

"Sounds right." Jaxton gulped down an entire glass of water before pouring himself another and chomped on some crackers.

I frowned and thought of the bond between the dragon and me and let out a breath. "I want to be able to shift. It's time, don't you think?"

Rome tilted his head. "Let's get sober. We can try it. Although I don't think your Rowen will be happy if you shift without her watching. I saw the way that she looked at you as a dragon. She's a fan."

I smiled. I couldn't help it. "I would ask how I got so lucky, but I don't think luck had anything to do with us. I'm just so fucking glad that the bond came back. I know I'll never be able to take back the feeling of what happened when the bond broke between us. And it did break." I paused and looked at them. "I also know that Rowen's already thought of this, but I don't know if I have it in me to confirm it to her face."

"What?" Rome asked, frowning.

"The bond between us is what triggered the curse in the first place. Without it, I don't know if my curse would've reacted the same way."

"I never want to be that person who says that maybe things happen for a reason, because fuck that. Fuck those reasons." Jaxton frowned. "But the bond's back. It shattered, but it's back. Without you having to do anything. I mean, it's not like you slept together in the interim, right?"

I looked between them and frowned. "We slept together the night before. Without my soul. I was a fucking asshole, and it was angry, it was hard, but it was what we both wanted. She wanted me, even in that instance when I wasn't myself. She wanted me. And I don't know what to do with that."

Jaxton blinked. "That means that you were meant. Always."

"Well then." Rome cleared his throat. "I wasn't expecting that. I mean, I knew you always had chemistry, even when she wanted to hate you. But hell."

That made me frown. "Wanted to hate me? No. She always hated me."

"No, I think that's the problem," Jaxton whispered, sounding far soberer. He was a shifter, so he would be able to work out the alcohol far easier than a human or even a witch could. Only I figured the conversation was easing this a bit more.

"You two had each other through the darkness, and now you're going to have to figure out how to fight beside each other and forgive one another. Because while Rowen is blameless for losing your soul, she was also still here.

Waiting. Even if she didn't want to be. To find the path. Find the way. And talk."

I puffed out my chest, sober once more. "First, I want to shift. I want to find my dragon, and then I will find how to go to my knees and beg forgiveness from the woman that I've always loved, even when I didn't know what love was."

"And along the way, defeat a necromancer, save the town, save the girl that you love, and maybe have a triple mating ceremony with all of us." Rome wiggled his brows, and I laughed. "Easier said than done. I mean, it's just a checklist, right?"

"Just a checklist," Jaxton agreed. "And let's get to shifting. Take off those clothes."

"See, and I bet you the girls would've wanted to see this. We should've invited them."

I shook my head at Rome's words. "Considering that Jaxton's mate is my sister, I'm going to go with a no on that."

I shuddered as Jaxton laughed. "Yes, there are some things that my mate does not need to see."

We all stripped to our skin, the moonlight glowing down on us, and I shook my head. "You know, outside of this town, or maybe even *within* this town, this is a mighty fucking weird sight. Three grown men with tattoos, naked as the day they were born, standing in a field behind a man's house."

"Hey, what happens in the privacy of a field behind a

man's house stays in the privacy of a field behind a man's house," Rome grumbled.

"Say that three times fast," I laughed.

"I could barely say it the first time, and I'm a bear, with bear tolerance for booze. Now, pull on that bond between you and your shifter, and feel the dragon. Be the dragon. Save the dragon."

"Are you quoting Miss Congeniality?" Jaxton asked.

Rome shrugged, his cheeks reddening. "Maybe. Or not. I saw it on the internet once. Get off my back."

"Well, be the dragon, I guess." Jaxton rolled his eyes.

"Be the dragon." I closed my eyes and focused on the bond between the dragon and me. I could feel my anchor weighing on my skin, warming as it moved around, getting to know me. I knew it wasn't a separate entity and it had to be part of me, but it was so new. I wasn't born with this, and I had only done it once before. I couldn't bring it forth. At least, I didn't think so. But I pulled, I focused on the dragon, and then I could breathe, as if something pulled at me, fire and warmth and coolness and dread and everything that came with life and honor and who I was pushed out of me, and I opened my eyes to see myself once again standing heads above the bear and the hawk. The hawk flew up, flying around my head, and I tilted my nose up, trying to bump it. I swore I saw it narrow its gaze at me before it landed on top of my head, and I let out a laugh, smoke billowing. The bear in front of me went to its back legs and glared at me, though I saw the laughter in its eyes, and so I leaned down, pressing my head to the ground as the hawk jumped off and then swirled above us.

We were shifters three, part of the coven somehow, and part of this Ravenwood that needed to be protected at all costs, because of the magic, because of the people, because of the legacy.

I looked over at the bear and the hawk and knew that the magic that Rowen had placed over me would hide me from others, just like the magic of Ravenwood would protect us, and so we would do the same for it. And so I stretched out my wings as the hawk did the same, and the bear roamed beside us, and we were three.

Shifters, connections.

Brothers. And friends.

We would avenge those we had lost. We would find answers to the questions left unspoken.

And we would find a way.

Because I loved a witch. I loved this town.

And I needed to find redemption. It was the only thing I had left.

CHAPTER

SIXTEEN

Rowen

"Wine, cheese, and spinach cups—I do believe we have a winner."

I looked over at Laurel as she clapped her hands in front of her and I shook my head. "There's spinach and cheese in filo cups. Technically it's just more cheese. We should probably have something other than cheese-covered spinach as a vegetable."

"I do have a crudités platter," Sage added as she walked in, said platter in her hands. "I won't let us eat only cheese. Although that does sound amazing."

"These are so scrummy," Laurel said, chopping down on a filo pastry.

I took one myself, popped it into my mouth, and groaned. "I am forever thankful for the day that we found this recipe. I could happily just eat the entire tray and go to sleep."

"If you eat this entire tray, there will be war," Laurel growled, holding up one finger. "After all, we must share the filo."

"I also made a rosemary focaccia," Sage added. "So, there's more than that for bread. And yeast rolls. And Cheshire rye rolls."

I groaned and held my stomach, though I couldn't wait to taste it all.

"How much bread do we actually need?" Laurel asked with a laugh.

I shook my head. "I'm a little worried about the number of carbs we're going to be eating, but that's fine with me. We need the energy." The girls gave me a look, and I shrugged. "The protein, the vegetables, the carbs, all of it gives me a little bit more energy to fight back. I'm going to be okay. We're going to find a way. After all, the ancestors told us we would be."

Sage let out a breath. "I cannot believe we spoke to the ancestors. The founders. It doesn't even seem real sometimes. This new life of mine. Of ours."

I smiled softly and reached across the table to squeeze

Sage's hand. "It doesn't seem real, but here we are. Making it so."

"I love you both so much. I just want you to know that."

"We love you too." I looked at my sisters of the heart and sighed.

Laurel frowned, staring between us. "I still don't know what we're supposed to do with the ancestors. At least with what they said. What needs to break or come down in order to build back up?"

I pressed my lips together at Laurel's words, worried. "I have a horrible feeling I know. But if that's the case, I don't know what happens after."

"The wards"? Sage asked, her train of thought clearly on the same path as mine.

I nodded. "If the wards need to come down, then how will we protect the town? How will we hide our magic from the outside world? How will we keep the revenants at bay?"

Laurel scowled. "And how will we protect you from fading, because you are connected to the wards?"

I took a Cheshire rye roll and tore in half, added Irish butter as the girls stared at me, waiting for my answer. I took a bite, letting the saltiness of the butter and the cheese settle on my tongue as the other flavors exploded. "First, I don't know but we will find out, damn it. Second, these are amazing, Sage. I'd ask for the recipe, but I don't believe even with all of my magic, I could ever be as good of a baker as you."

"My magic for peace and even my anxiety are in these rolls," Sage mumbled. "You're a wonderful baker, Rowen. You know that."

I smiled. "I'm not. I'm adequate. I can follow a recipe. But you were the one with the shine and the talents. It was what you were always meant to be. As for the wards...I'm not only connected to the entity protecting this town. Yes, they're draining me, but I'm also connected to the core in town. If the wards fall, I have to hope that I'm strong enough to survive the whiplash."

Sage paled even as Laurel spoke, her fire dancing in her eyes. "And we'll be there right beside you making sure that doesn't happen. We've already added more magic and spells to strengthen the wards, so it's not just on you. It will fall onto *all* of us. Onto the fae, onto the shifters. Everyone. It will not just be you."

I heard the desperation in Laurel's tone, and I understood it. "I just haven't had time to settle. To truly think. Everything is happening so fast, and yet it feels like we've been waiting for this time for years."

"Are you speaking of the darkness of prophecy, or my brother?" Laurel asked, her teeth worrying her lip.

I blinked at the sudden change in tone. I leaned against the antique armchair and looked around the home that had kept me safe for so long. There were so many memories here and I was so worried we weren't going to be around long enough to make more. "I don't know. That's odd to think. I don't know."

Laurel leaned forward and squeezed my hand, the strength giving me hope. She'd once been so weak because of the curse, but now she was a pillar of strength. It made me want to weep in gratitude. "He's back, and you two have just fallen in together once more, and I could not be happier. But I'm also worried for both of you."

I took a sip of my wine, then gulped the rest down, noticing Sage's wince. "No more wine for me. Just that one. I need to keep on my toes these days. However, Ash and I haven't just fallen into this. We're trying to figure out who we are now rather than the people that we had once been or the people that we turned into along the way. It's complicated, but we are talking, and we're *mated*. The bond is there. It came back without even trying. As soon as his soul was retrieved, it came back to us."

"It's beautiful. That you two were always meant to be. Even when fate pushed you apart." Sage wiped a tear, and I swallowed hard.

"I loved him. All this time, I loved him. And that's why it hurts. Because he was a horrible person—that's what he tells me at least, and that's what we saw in evidence throughout the years. Even when I knew sometimes he tried not to be because there had to be part of him still there, he pushed people away, and he hurt others." I let out a breath. "And I wasn't nice either."

Laurel scowled. "Rowen. That's not true. About you at

least. Ash is reconciling with the man he was without a soul, but you weren't on that path."

I wasn't so sure and that worried me. "I was horrible to Ash. I lashed out because I hated that he was back, that he was here. I wouldn't let him be part of the coven because I was breaking. That's on me. That's my own selfishness."

Laurel stood up and paced, her anger her shield as always. "We all know that he couldn't truly be part of the coven like he's becoming now without a soul. Yes, he had the magic, but he didn't have the connections needed. You weren't an asshole."

"I was. Because I was hurting. I don't want to hurt anymore when it comes to him. I love him. I do. I don't know what's going to happen next with us, or even the coven. All I know is that we need to work together, and that means I need to allow myself to feel. Something I haven't been doing for so long."

It was odd to think that so much had changed over the years and yet, in some respects, we were right back to where we started. None of it made sense and yet all of it almost seemed preordained.

"And you have to fall in love with the man that he is, and not just who he was." Sage reached out and squeezed my hand. "I know you love him. I can feel it in the magic in the air. I can *feel* it. Now you can enrich that love."

"But first, we need to save the world." My best friend held up her glass in a mock toast.

I laughed at Laurel's words. "No problem. We can

pencil that in for Tuesday and then on Wednesday, maybe I could try to forgive myself for not letting myself live for all these years. I mean, I was becoming the old spinster witch in the haunted house rather than a real human."

"How were you supposed to live when part of your soul was taken right along with him?" Sage asked, the silence afterward deafening. My heart raced and I pushed those feelings aside, worried about where they would lead me and if I was ready to face them at all.

"Enough about me," I said after a moment. "I just need to breathe, and just listen to y'all and have answers for you, rather than be all questions."

Sage smiled. "I can tell you a story about the triplets, the three baby cubs that are trying into get into more mischief than I ever thought possible."

Laurel grinned. "You know, Trace, Jaxton, and Rome were like that too. Always getting into trouble. Two baby bears and a baby hawk." My heart clutched as I looked at Laurel, who just shrugged. "Alden was there too, of course. The triplet bears were just like the current triplet bears. But Jaxton was part of them too. And Ash, of course."

I grinned. "The five of them were rough and tumble."

"We held our own alongside them." Laurel beamed.

"I hate that magic and circumstance kept me away for so long." Sage let out a breath. "I loved my husband. I loved the life that I had, even though it wasn't easy. And when I lost him, I thought it all was over, and it hurts to think that Oriel and his magic were part of that. Part of losing him, part of losing myself. But now that I'm here, I'm going to find happiness no matter what we do."

Both Laurel and I reached out and squeezed Sage's hands. "We're here for you. I promise." I smiled softly, knowing I needed to find the positivity like Sage.

Laurel leaned back, tilted her head. "I say we eat, drink, and just enjoy tonight for what we can."

"Seriously though, the baby bears got into the honey cabinet. In my shop." Sage threw her hands up, making Laurel and me laugh.

I sipped my water, taking a bite of cheese that made my mouth water. "How much trouble are they in?"

"They didn't get into any of the priceless things and were very, very careful for tiny bears with tiny claws. All they did was open up the large jar of honey and go to town. It was thankfully my bonus honey—the honey that I use just in case a bear comes in and wants so much honey that they don't care if it's organic or from a special hive or not."

"At least they were smart baby bears," Laurel said with a laugh.

"Smart baby bears are going to make me tear my hair out," Sage added, shaking her head.

We talked more about baby bears and mating ceremonies. However, we did very well about not mentioning Ash or me anymore. We hadn't had a mating ceremony before. We'd only been mated for a day, the bond fresh and new before it has been torn asunder.

However, there was happiness. There was joy. There was Nelle's healing in her relationship with Aspen. There was Esmeralda slowly finding love with a bear shifter with a kind heart. There was Ariel, the beta for the bears, becoming pregnant again. There was life and change and chance. All of that was what we were fighting for. Not just the magic that could change the scope of the world. But it was the lives and the families and the choices that we were making that brought who we were together.

And who we would fight for.

The wards outside my house fluctuated a bit, and I frowned, slowly sitting up as I sat down a pastry that I made for the evening.

Laurel tilted her head, her senses on alert as she stood, sword in hand. Sage looked between us, closed her eyes, then opened them wide as she leaned down, picked up her metal bat, and nodded tightly.

"Someone's out there. Someone who was able to get through the town wards but couldn't get through my home wards."

"Can you tell who it is?"

I nodded at Laurel's question. "Yes. And you're not going to like the answer."

Flame danced in her eyes. Her phoenix rose to the surface, and her body shimmered before staying in its human form. "Renee."

Oriel's lieutenant. A fire witch necromancer who had lost her mate, Jaxton's cousin. The woman had also nearly killed Jaxton and Laurel and twisted up the wards enough with her own strength that I was truly afraid of what this woman wanted.

"She's here for me," Laurel growled, her arm aflame.

I shook my head, my own anger rising to the surface with my wind magic. "Or me, or Sage, or anybody for revenge. We took her mate. And we nearly killed her."

"Well, it looks like I'm going to finish the damned job," Laurel growled.

Sage nodded tightly. "I pushed on the bonds towards Rome and Jaxton, but let's do this."

I looked at them, at my coven, and rolled my shoulders back. "Let's go."

I pushed at the bond towards Ash, something I hadn't even thought to do because it wasn't second nature to me yet. I had ignored it for so long, had done so well pretending that I didn't love him, that I didn't want him, that even asking for help now was foreign to me.

But I would do it. For him. For me. For us. Warmth and love seeped across the bond back to me, and I relished that. Clung to it. This would give me strength. As long as I told myself that, I would not relinquish that strength.

We stepped outside and down the porch, magic thrumming through the air. Renee stood on the edge of the property line, her hair pulled back in a tight braid, her leather jacket and jeans frayed. She had a scar on her face, and her hand was twisted slightly from the burns. I felt no pity for her. I tried. I truly did. For the loss she must have sustained, for the pain she must have been in. But she had lost her connection to her soul and what was good long ago. She tortured and tried to kill those I loved.

It was only the magic of who Laurel and Jaxton were that had saved them. It wasn't anything I had done or could have done.

Renee had been the catalyst to bring it all to flame and ash. She was part of the power trying to kill my town and my family. I did not pity her. Maybe that made me a bad person, but I was done trying to be the better person for those trying to kill my family.

"Such silly wards," Renee teased, her voice a little scratchy, as if she had inhaled too much smoke.

"They kept you back, didn't they?" Laurel snapped.

"For now. But it was so easy to slide through the wards of the town, as if they weren't even there. And yet, all you can do is stand there behind your pretty witch wards here and not even face me. I wonder what would happen if I were to press my magic or my revenants through your boundaries. Would they hurt you? I know that touching the town wards with anything other than the casualness of magics hurts you, Ravenwood. I want you to hurt. I want you to feel pain. I want you to feel everything that I do. So, you will just have to stand there and take what I give you."

"Are you done with the villain talk?" Sage asked, her voice sounding bored, though I knew there was anger and fear underneath the casualness. "It's ridiculous. You're not even making any sense. All you do is talk in circles, and yet, look at you. You barely made it out last time. Do you really think you're going to be able to fight the three of us?"

Renee just grinned, and a sense of foreboding slid down my spine. "Who says that I'm alone?"

She snapped her fingers and revenants slid out of the trees. Only they weren't the crawling drooling messes that they were before. No, these were nearly sentient. Renee's control over them unimaginable. Oriel had done it before when he encircled me, revealing who he was. And now Renee had that power as well.

How many dark sacrifices, how many souls had they had to rip from another in order to make that happen?

I swallowed down my bile at the thought, and nearly fell off the porch when I realized what two of the revenants were dragging between them.

"Esmeralda," I whispered, my voice dry. Fear slammed into me, and I nearly let me magic out—knowing it would be futile in this instant with Renee having the upper hand.

She looked up at me then, one eye swollen shut, her lip bleeding, her legs were broken, twisted masses dragged behind her. The pain and fear in her eyes nearly broke me. Laurel held me back, only because if I had moved even further, I would've been led into the trap. Because Renee was ready, a magic fireball in her hand and a wicked grin on her face.

"We found your little witch. You're not as strong as you should be. As strong as you think you are. It took nothing at all for us to take her."

"Oh no," Sage whispered, her hand going mouth. However, her other hand tightened on the handle of the bat. She was ready to fight, but we were outnumbered. The only way we could win this was by touching dark magic, and that was a line we could not cross.

"You left your witch unsafe. Of course, can we really call her that? She's practically human with the amount of magic in her veins. It's a little ridiculous that you keep calling these little people witches when they don't even have the power that I have in my pinky." Renee reached out, slid her hand over Esmeralda's shoulders, and squeezed, flame dancing along her skin. Esmeralda screamed, and I moved forward, slashing at my hand. An air dagger cut off the head of one revenant, the body falling down on the other side of Esmeralda and Renee.

"You are predictable. But don't you worry. I'll make it easy. Give us the town's core, make it simple, and your little friend here will live. If not, it's one less weak witch for you to protect."

"How about I take my friend back, and you scream in agony as you die?" I asked, knowing I couldn't give the core to Renee. No matter what, I *couldn't*.

And from the look of sorrow in Esmeralda's eyes, she understood. I looked at my friend, the woman who had been part of my shop for years, and I hoped she saw the determination in my gaze. I was not going to let Esmeralda get hurt any more than she had. I would make it better. I would make it all better.

I moved forward, ready to strike out, but Renee just smiled and twisted her hand up, the flame turning purple. I screamed, throwing my magic out, the same as Sage and Laurel. Laurel's fire danced along the flame, and Renee moved out of the way, but not before Esmeralda screamed, and then there was silence. Her neck at an odd angle.

My friend, my fellow witch, and the woman I had been chosen to protect, lay on the ground, her body broken but no longer in pain.

Tears didn't threaten. I had none left. I screamed, power erupting. The core beneath my feet rumbled, ready to reach out to aid, but I pushed it back, knowing I couldn't rely on it. I couldn't use this magic or risk going onto the dark side. I held up my hands, palms outstretched, and called forth the magic of my ancestors.

Air thrummed within me, and I pushed out, slamming into the revenants. They fell one by one, and Sage used her bat and her water magic to kill the rest. Laurel aided Sage while she ran towards Renee, sword outstretched. Renee pulled out her own sword and fought against Laurel, blade against blade, fire against fire.

But now, I could not let this be only Laurel's fight. I walked over the dead revenants, over the people who had once been alive and thriving, moved towards Renee, and screamed. The air froze as if the magic was too much for it, and Renee turned me slowly, and I held up my hand and pulled, squeezing my hand into a fist. Her eyes widened, and then they bulged. She dropped the sword, clung to her neck, and Laurel staggered back, staring at me. Sage clutched Laurel's hand as they looked at me and as I squeezed my own fist tighter. Renee clung to her neck, her fingernails digging into her skin, but I tugged, and I pulled, and I leeched. I pulled every ounce of air from her body, sliding it from her. Her skin sunk into itself, her body caving in, and she tried to scream, but she had no air at all.

I looked at Laurel and nodded, and my friend didn't look at me in horror. No, she met my gaze with understanding, and she took her sword and neatly sliced Renee's head off. A clean slice, for we did not torture, we did not enjoy the kill.

But I was glad that this woman was dead.

And as the others came through the forest, taking out the last of the revenants who might have tried to escape, Ash, Rome, Frank, Jaxton, and Aspen all there to aid, I let the others do what they needed to. I fell to my knees, held Esmeralda to my chest, and I screamed.

CHAPTER

SEVENTEEN

Ash

I sat in an armchair next to Rowen's bed, coffee in hand, and I watched the love of my life sleep. She had dark circles under her eyes, and I wasn't sure she was gaining anything from the sleep at this point, since she had passed out from the power drain, the grief, and just pure exhaustion from the cleanup and planning after the attack at her home.

But the yard was clean, Esmeralda had been buried—her body first turned to ash so she could not be turned into a revenant, but the anguish was still overwhelming, and I wasn't sure that Rowen would be able to make the choices needed for later. Or even agree with the choices she had already made.

I had come too late to the fight to see it all, but I had seen the magic she had used, the spell she had taken from the ancestors to take out Renee. It drew far too much power, one that could nearly take any other witch to the dark, but it hadn't this time. It had only brought out the grief more.

Esmeralda, the sweet witch who loved what she did, and though she didn't use magic could light up the room with her smile lined black lipstick. She made everyone else laugh along with her.

I had seen her for who she was. Rowen's friend. And Renee had known that. And she had used it. But Renee was gone. I wondered if Oriel had used her as cannon fodder. To breach the wards again as a test. Knowing that Renee wouldn't be able to last for long.

I sipped my coffee and ignored the bitter taste, knowing that it was my mood, not the beans, that made it that way. I set the mug down on the nightstand, leaned back on the chair, and watched my mate sleep. It hurt. Everything hurt. I couldn't protect her. I couldn't do what I needed to in order to make her better.

My heart felt far too heavy for the decisions that needed to be made soon.

We were at the end of our rope. All of us knew it. Something needed to change. We needed a stronger power that came from more than the coven itself. All we were doing was reacting and not fighting forward or being on the offensive. We didn't have the power that he did. And it worried me. Because I wasn't sure how we were supposed to fight without using magic that was stronger than Oriel's. He'd had decades to enact his plan, to fold into his magic and create revenants and wait for this moment. In contrast, we had been shattered and had to piece ourselves together, slowly coming forward.

I wasn't sure where we would find the strength to be stronger.

"You're thinking so hard that I can practically feel it along the bond." I looked up to see Rowen awake, her eyes sleepy, her hair spilled over the pillow. I leaned forward and traced my fingertips along her skin.

"I didn't mean to wake you."

"The sun is up. I can feel the magic shining along my skin. It is time for me to get out of bed."

I shook my head. "No, it's really not. It's time for you to let me kiss you."

She smiled then and shook her head. "That just seems like an excuse."

I sighed, ran my fingers along her skin. I couldn't not touch her. "The frequency of the attacks is increasing. The magic pools are draining. I think that it's time to kiss you. To be with you. Because I don't believe we're going to have a lot of time after this."

She swallowed hard at the starkness of my words and reached forward, tugging at my shoulders.

"Then be with me, Ash. Let's just forget for a moment. I need to forget."

"And then we'll talk. We'll plan. And we'll avenge. Everything. Everything these curses, this town, and Oriel has done. We'll avenge." I wasn't just speaking of the prophecy, or of my own magic, or losing Esmeralda. I was speaking of everything. And as she maneuvered me over her, I knew she understood as well.

The sheet lay between us, far too thin. Though she was already naked, and I wore sweatpants and a t-shirt, I still was grateful for the sheet, just for now so we could go slow. I dropped kisses along her skin, along her chin, and then down her neck. And when I gently pulled the blanket down, she let me, her smile soft, a woman who knew what she wanted. Her breasts lay bare before me and I slid my hand around one globe, flicked my tongue over her nipple, and she hummed.

"Sex magic is supposed to replenish your stores far quicker than anything else."

"That's what I hear," I mumbled before I went to her other breast, sucking and licking. "I suppose I better make sure that I love you right, to give you all the energy that you need. Just in case."

"For the science, of course," she whispered, and I pressed her breasts together, kissing both before letting them fall, the action getting a giggle out of her.

"Ash."

"I always did love to play with my food before I ate."

She blushed all the way to those nipples of hers, and I kissed her again before slowly licking and nipping down her chest and her stomach. I kissed the valley between her breasts again and then nibbled around her belly button. She giggled, wriggling under me, but I pinned her down before pulling the sheet all the way off her.

She was all curves and sin and mine. She had a small thatch of curls between her legs the same color as her hair, dark, inviting, and so when I spread her thighs, her glistening cunt calling to me, I moved down and licked along her clit. She moaned, cupping her breasts as she arched for me, and I spread her lower lips, licking and sucking and kneading. She was pink and ready, and I knew I could enter her right then, fucking her hard, and she would love every minute of it, but first I needed to have her, just mine. And so, I ate and sucked, and I filled her with myself, and when she came, she whispered my name, and the magic in the air pulsated, thrilling, and connecting us on a deeper level than ever before.

I stripped down before I settled myself between her thighs. Then I met her gaze, the gray of hers dark with need, and I slid deep inside. She was slick, wet, hot. And her pussy clamped around my cock like a vice. We made love slow, and when I rolled to my back, letting her ride me, the lights flickered, the air swirled, and the house shook. I could feel the magic within me soaring, increasing with every thrust and roll of her hips.

Sex magic was the deepest magic and only worked

when it came from a place of hope. And this was my mate. My destiny.

I would protect Rowen at all costs. And when she came again, I followed her and pulled her down to me, needing her lips on mine.

We kissed, and we came, the orgasm filling our magical stores to the brink.

And she grinned down at me, her body shaking.

"I've never felt this much magic before. Not even touching the core of the town."

I thrust up into her again.

"I could make a joke about your core filling me up, but isn't it the other way around?"

She laughed and shoved at my shoulder, even while she was still clamped around me. "You're ridiculous."

"Yes, I am. But I'm also a guy. Of course, I'm going to make dick jokes."

We lay there, both of us coming down off our high, and she slid her hands down my body. "We should clean up and then go do our check of the wards."

Reality settled in, but I needed this moment—as if we both knew we wouldn't get another one until the end. "We still have another hour until it's our shift."

"I know. I just want to get out there. I have a bad feeling. Like yesterday was just the beginning."

I nodded, swallowing hard. "You're not alone." I kissed one temple, then the other. "Let's shower, get you fed, and then we'll begin our day."

"Oriel's been planning this for so long, and we're just not catching up. What if we're not strong enough?"

I frowned as I pulled her into the shower, turning the taps to hot. "This doesn't sound like you. You're always the one of strength and of knowing our purpose."

"She killed Esmeralda because she was there. And she tortured her. You saw her legs, saw her face. And I didn't even know. I was having a girl's night with the coven, enjoying ourselves and talking about you and boys and the cubs. We were just laughing and enjoying ourselves while Esmeralda was screaming in pain. And I couldn't even feel it. Oriel was blocking me so much I couldn't even feel it. The wards are twisted. They're his now. And that's what worries me. I was laughing when my friend was dying. And I wasn't even aware of it."

I cursed under my breath, anger radiating inside of me. "You didn't know. You can't be everywhere at all times."

"Maybe I should be. Why wasn't I strong enough to do this? Why did I almost lose everything once again? Esmeralda did lose everything. It's not right. Like maybe I wasn't the right person for this. Maybe someone else should've been the leader."

"That's bullshit. And you know it."

Her eyes narrowed. "Maybe not. Maybe Sage should be the strongest one. She's the steady one now. Laurel's just finding herself, and I keep screwing up."

She washed her hair quickly, almost angrily, as I

growled beside her. "You brought me back. You've brought all of us back. You don't need to do it all alone. We're here for you."

"And yet Oriel keeps winning."

I held her close as she cried, knowing it was more out of anger than despair just then. And then we got out of the shower and dressed, not bothering to dry our hair. There wasn't much time, and when Rowen just shook her head and whispered a spell under her breath that took no magic at all, the air within the home dried us.

I snorted. "I forgot you knew how to do that."

"It's second nature now. I don't want to catch a cold, after all."

I shook my head, sighing at the sadness in her voice, and we made our way to Main Street to begin our shift. None of us were working now. Our shops were all closed, and even the tourists weren't venturing in and out anymore. It was as if in the past week things had shifted abruptly, and we hadn't even fully been cognizant of it until it had almost been too late.

"Something's coming; I can feel it." Her voice carried on the wind, as if her magic amplified her tone.

I frowned as I looked at her. "What's coming?"

"I don't know, but I'm worried. Why do I feel like last night was a test?" She frowned. "A test we failed."

"You're not alone," Laurel said as she walked forward, Jaxton by her side. Her sword was strapped to her back, no magic even concealing it. And that's when I looked around and realized that the only people in town were that of Ravenwood. Not a single tourist at all.

"Is Oriel keeping the others out?" I asked abruptly.

Jaxton shook his head. "Perhaps. I think it's the wards themselves."

"They're not ours anymore." Rowen looked up, frowned, and looked around. "The wards aren't ours anymore. Oh my god, that's what he's been doing all this time—testing the wards, weaving his magic in and out. That's why it's draining. They're his."

Sage and Rome were there then, frowning. "His? How can that be?" The little witch looked around us and we all studied the magic we could feel.

"Because I am Ravenwood. And now the town is mine." Oriel spoke from the other side of the bridge, and we turned, readying to fight, but then Rowen nearly fell, shouting. Revenant after revenant, dozens of them stood with Oriel. Only, it wasn't what pushed in, what echoed through all of us.

It was the other members of Ravenwood, coming out of their homes, of their businesses, the town rocked on its core, and the wards did what they'd threatened to do for an eternity.

They fell.

EIGHTEEN

Rowen

Agony ripped up my arms, down my sides, through my heart. Perhaps even around my soul as it tore from my body and slammed back in.

The wards were gone.

And I was going with them.

"No! Not now. Not fucking right now."

Ash's words echoed in my head, and I pushed at the pain, pushed at the darkness. I needed to be stronger than this. I needed to come back.

To Ash.

To Ravenwood.

To myself.

The wards were gone, as was my connection to them, and it felt as if I were an open siphon, my body and soul draining from a jagged wound.

But something else was there.

Something I hadn't expected.

The core.

The core of Ravenwood was waiting for me. The power, the strength, and the daunting menace that was the strength of a people from eons past mixed with the intensity of a town well-made.

It clung to me.

It saved me.

And if I weren't careful, it would kill me.

I fisted my hands and focused, trying to slow my breathing. The others were shouting around me, a thousand things going on all at once but, in order to help, I needed to be strong. I needed to get myself out of this. I pulled on the core, on the magic that Oriel wanted, and I hoped to hell I wasn't going to take too much.

The center of the town seemed so young and yet aged at the same time. As if it had seen everything and yet hadn't experienced it itself. It wrapped around me, giving me strength, and I told myself I would do the same for it.

"I will protect you," I whispered, but I wasn't even sure the words were coming out of my mouth rather than just in my head. "I will protect you at all costs."

The core seemed almost to hug me, as if it were a

young child, coming to terms with who he was. Or who they were. I sucked in a breath, the pain excruciating as the wards fell completely, shattering into mist. Over a century's worth of power and protection gone in an instant.

My eyes opened as the core of the town held me strong, as did the man holding me. Ash's arms were bands of steel around me, his eyes blazing with his dragon as he tried to keep me steady. He knelt on the ground as I splayed on top of him, the others of the coven around us for protection.

"Rowen," he growled, his voice far deeper than normal. It was the shifter in him, the one he was longing to control, just as I was trying to control what was inside me.

"The wards are gone. Completely." My voice was far stronger than I thought it would be, but I knew it wasn't just mine. No, it was the core of the town trying to protect me, just like I had been trying to do the same for it all this time.

Ash's eyes widened for a moment before he nodded tightly. "We could feel it."

"Help me up." I needed to stand up, to be on my own. To not show weakness. The town depended on me, and I was tired of bleeding and falling in front of it.

"We should be staying down," Sage said, worry in her tone.

I shook my head, then shoved at Ash slightly so I

could get up on my own two feet. I let him help me, but the magic thrumming through me was stronger than any magic I'd ever felt before in my life.

This was why Oriel wanted the power. I was far stronger than I had ever been, and it was because of the power of combined magics settled underneath our feet. I didn't know how long it would last or what would happen if I relied on it to keep me steady for longer than a few more minutes. But this was what Oriel wanted. And I knew without a doubt he couldn't have it. He would twist it, he would taint it, and he would harm the rest of the world using it. And I couldn't let him bastardize this.

I stood on my own two feet, sucking in a breath as I looked around my town, and I knew this was the beginning of the end, this was the darkness that had been foretold, and we were too late.

"Oriel took over the wards. He's been doing it all this time but hiding it when he attacks. And it's not as if we've been able to stop him completely. If we'd seen what he had been doing, we wouldn't have been able to save the town from the revenants. He's had years in order to plan this, and we weren't ready."

Laurel's eyes blazed, a fire within dancing. "What do we do now? Can we build new wards?"

I let out a shaky breath, coming slowly aware of my surroundings. "My answer would have been no before this because we couldn't build on what was already there, but now it's gone. First, we need to protect the town, or see to what's left of it." I looked around as people screamed.

Because the town of Ravenwood was no longer protected from the outside world. Shifters and witches and fae would be able to be seen by humans, those who would be kind, and those who would be scared—those who would see us as a way to their own power. There were reasons that we hid from the humans and the government and everyone else that could hurt us.

"We need a plan," Jaxton stated as he looked around, as if we were waiting for the revenants to come through at any moment. Only they weren't. The wards were down, and the revenants weren't piling through.

Why? That was the question.

"Oriel has done this because he wants to destabilize the town. He wants to take power from the core itself. I'm not going to let that happen." I looked at all of them and swallowed hard. "The wards are down, but I'm still standing. Not because of my own magic, but because the core is protecting me."

Ash's eyes narrowed. "Explain."

I ignored his tone because it sounded much like it had when he hadn't had his soul, but I knew he was scared for me. I was scared right along with him. "The core of the town wrapped itself around me, and it's keeping me protected. And I'm going to do the same for it."

"You can't take on that much power," Laurel chided. "If

you do, it'll overwhelm you. You don't know what will happen."

I raised my chin, the power nearly deafening, but then it ebbed away, as if it knew I needed to be in the one in control for now. "I know this. I'm not siphoning any. At least, I don't think so. We don't have time for this. I will protect it at all costs, but we need to make sure that we protect this town."

I opened my mouth to say something else, but then my ears began to ring. The bridge in front of us exploded, concrete and brick and stone shattering everywhere. I was thrown off my feet as I tried to lift my hands to summon magic, only I was flying, my body slamming into the ground. Sage was closest, and I screamed for her. Rome threw his body over her as a stone slab slammed into his back. He shouted, the roar of a bear shattering two closed windows.

Sage had her arm around him and yet had one hand free in order to pull the water from the river and created a barricade. Not a ward, but a wall of water that stopped the rest of the stone and rock and part of the bridge from hitting any innocent bystanders.

I slammed into the ground, my hands bloody as I scraped along the pavement. I scrambled up, Ash pulling at me. I wiped away the blood from his eyebrow and then nearly let out a choked sob as I looked over at Rome. He lay sprawled on the ground. Terror filled me and bile coated my throat.

Rome's chest wasn't moving.

"No!" Sage screamed. She put her hands on him and cried out. "No. We're not doing this. You're going to be okay."

Love, passion, hope, and desperation wrapped around her, and the core of the town pulsated through me before it shot along the bond that made us coven and into Sage. Sage's eyes widened, her hair flowing around her before the core's magics pulled out of her and into Rome.

Rome, the bear shifter who lay prone on the grounds, not moving, not breathing. I couldn't focus. I couldn't understand what was happening. All I knew was that Rome wasn't breathing. And his back was broken, his body shattered. And he had protected Sage while she had protected us.

I hadn't been strong enough.

Rome couldn't be gone. This couldn't be happening.

Rome was not dead.

Only Sage was screaming. *Screaming.*

Jaxton and Laurel left us. They've left to protect the others and pull some of the innocent out of the way as I ran towards Sage.

The core of the town shot out of her, a wave of magic that nearly rocked me off my feet and into Ash. And as Sage cried and screamed, Rome let in a shocked breath, and I nearly fell to my knees.

I...I couldn't focus. I couldn't do anything but stare at

the bear was who was my friend and brother and wonder what the hell I had just done.

"Did the core of the town just bring him back?" Ash whispered, awe and fear in his tone.

I swallowed hard. "I think so. Oh my god. Did he...?" I couldn't even finish the statement.

Rome had died.

Rome had died. And yet, the core had brought him back. He moved slowly as if he were trying to figure out how he could even move at all, and Sage was sobbing, holding him close.

And I wanted to reach them, run to them and try to figure out what had just happened, but I couldn't.

Because the war had only just begun.

Another explosion rocked beside us, and the town library erupted into flames, before crumbling down and on itself. I screamed, then shoved my air forward, pushing the roof up as two patrons and the librarian escaped.

"Was there anyone else in there?" I asked the bear shifter.

The older woman shook her head, her eyes glowing gold. "No, we got them all out. Rome. I felt him leave us." Her voice shook. That old stern librarian, who never sounded as if anything fazed her, but I heard the pain in her voice.

"I'm fine, Edna," Rome whispered as he came forward and held her close.

The older woman held him back slightly, patted his

back, and pushed him away. "Good. Never do that again. But our alpha's mate is strong. She protected you. Now, before I break down and blubber like a mess, which we do not have time for, what do we need, what do you need us to do?"

They all looked to me, even Ash, and I told myself I could do this. I had been leading this town, even more so than the mayor, for years. I could do this, and it was what we had been training for.

Although I hadn't quite expected it to end like this. I needed to focus on what I could do and not what was lost. "Rome, can we get the innocents and those who need help to the den? Will they be safe there?"

The alpha nodded, the determination in his gaze that of the alpha and not the man. "They will. Edna, find Ariel. She's at the end of the road with the wolves, get the innocents to the den. And protect them."

"Yes, sir, alpha. And never die again. I did not like that feeling." She nodded tightly before taking the hands of the two younger patrons by her side and running towards where Ariel was stationed.

Jaxton came forward, his gaze on Rome even as he spoke to all of us. "I'm going to go down to the other side, uptown, to protect what I can. Because right now, it is just Aspen there with Nelle."

I looked at Jaxton and nodded tightly. "Go. Protect the north side. Rome and Sage, go protect the west side."

Laurel raised her chin. "I'll take the east side."

"Not alone, you won't," Jaxton growled.

"She won't be alone," Frank the jaguar said as he came forward, three teenage wolves beside him.

The eldest with the scent of alpha cleared his throat. "We'll help. We're strong." They looked at Rome, lowered their gazes. "If that's okay, alpha."

The wolves had been integrated into the bear den, and Rome was their alpha. While I was the leader here, Rome was the one who would tell them what to do. And, in all honesty, I wasn't sure I could send three teenage boys to certain deaths.

But I also couldn't let Rome be the one to do it. Not when it came to death and decisions. Not right now. This was my responsibility. Even if I was afraid the others would resent me for it. I met the alpha's gaze, and he nodded tightly. "Go. Listen to Frank. We trained for this. You understand what to do."

They nodded before they turned on their heels and left, following Frank to the east side.

Ash stood beside me as another explosion rocked, as if fire and air and earth and water were all being used at once. "He has more necromancers than we knew," Ash whispered.

I nodded tightly. "And the wards were his. They've been his longer than I'd ever thought."

"That's why you've been so sick."

Realization settled into me, the pieces coming together. "I know. We're going to have to find a way."

"And we will."

And then the revenants came. Ash kissed me hard on the mouth, and I tried to tell myself it wasn't a final kiss. It couldn't be. But I wasn't sure.

The townspeople poured out of their homes, out of their dens and stores, witches with some magic, little sachets of spells in their hands, and weapons in their others. All shifters who weren't protecting their children or the weak were there, fighting hand-to-hand, protecting in their sectors of the town. I knew the fae were fighting, as was anybody that was able.

But something was off. The shifters were strong, the fae were strong, but we witches only had our coven. And that had to change.

We needed to find a way to be as strong as we had once been. We needed more magic. But this was not the time to find it. Not when the power of Oriel was so strong that he needed to have all my focus.

I took the sword from Ash, wondering where he had conjured it from, and then sliced the head off a revenant. It fell in front of me, but then another one came, and another one. The bridge was gone, our last protection on the south side from whatever Oriel brought.

These revenants and whoever else he had could walk into the town at any part, and I wouldn't be able to feel it.

We needed to build the ward back up. But first, we need to protect the town.

I sliced through the other revenants, then fell to my

knees as another explosion rocked. This time the town hall shattered, bricks falling. I pushed out with my air magic, creating a tunnel, making sure that none of the stone or anything else from the building could hurt others. A bear shifter shook off a piece of wood, nodded its head at me, and ran back into the fray, and I had to wonder who had done that. Was it Oriel? Or someone I didn't recognize? I didn't know, but we were losing. Our entire town was fighting with all that we had, but we didn't have enough of something. And that needed to change.

Oriel stepped out of the smoke in his dark suit, and a wicked grin on his face. But he didn't say anything. He held out his hands, and I wanted to weep. Right there, I wanted to break down. Because it wasn't necromancers he was using. It wasn't their magic. No, it was those of the lost. It was the magic of the necromancers lost that he was using.

Of Faith, of Renee. Of those, I didn't recognize. Of shifters who had been murdered. They weren't revenants.

No, these were shades.

Twisted and tortured souls that he could siphon their magic from, and he could attack.

Shades.

Something of legend, something so grotesque that if they touched you, they could siphon out your life force and kill you instantly.

A bear shifter screamed, one short scream, and then

was down, Faith the shade grinning like Oriel. I didn't know if Faith knew what she was doing, if that part of her soul understood. I didn't even understand how he could have gotten their shades to begin with. But Oriel was smart. And he had access to power and dark magic that we never would.

And we were going to lose.

"Give it up, dear sister. Give me the core of the town, or I'll take the next one. And the next one. I will make the town suffer for your hubris."

Tears spilled down my cheeks even as the rage burned within me. "Never. You will never have this town and never have this power."

"I will never let you have this magic," Ash growled beside me.

"You're weak. Your soul makes you weak. You're not even as strong enough as the bitch at your side. And yet you think you can take me? You're nothing."

He pushed out Renee, her shade screaming towards us. I put up a wall of air, but she slid right through. There was nothing to fight against the shade. We would die here. We would perish even as we fought for our lives.

The air around us simmered as Ash moved forward and roared. Before I could blink, Ash threw his head back and shifted. A dragon stood before us, protecting, waiting. I hadn't even realized he was going to do it, and he roared. Fear slammed into me, and I wanted to pull him back. Ash could *not* sacrifice himself for us.

Not after all we lost.

Flame erupted, and Renee backed off, the shade screaming back into Oriel. I saw Oriel's eyes flash for a moment, but I didn't know if it was surprise or anger. All I knew was that another building exploded, crumbling to dust.

People were screaming. We were dying. And we weren't powerful enough. And then, as quickly as it began, Oriel was gone, taking his shades with him. And I stood, looking at the dragon in front of me, who had just fought off a shade somehow, and then out at my town. Or what was left of it.

Ravenwood was falling.

We had lost.

And I wasn't sure what to do next.

CHAPTER
NINETEEN

Rowen

The town was burning. Not all of it, but enough of the structures and memories had burned or crumbled that it hurt my heart. Ash's dragon had pushed away the shades, at least for the moment, and Oriel wasn't taking up more of the town or coming at us yet. For now, we had a break as we stood in a field, the stars above us, the air soothing my aching soul.

And we were about to do something that had been on my mind for far too long, something that would change the landscape of Ravenwood forever. Something I hoped would finally come to fruition, even if it seemed beyond farfetched.

"Do you think that Oriel is taking a break from attacking us head-on as much as he has been because of his use of the shades?" Ash asked, bringing me out of my thoughts.

I turned to my mate, my other half, and swallowed hard. "That's where my thoughts were tracking. Using shades..." I shook my head. "That's controlling souls, not vessels, not even making revenants. That is controlling a soul and pulling it from the other world, from wherever our souls end up with the goddess."

Ash slid his hand down my back as we both thought through the events. "And it takes the darkest of necromancy to make that happen. It has to take strength. So much strength from the user."

"I only wish that it took enough of it that it killed him," Laurel grumbled as she came up to us.

I nodded at my best friend and wrapped my arm around her waist, squeezing her tight. "I don't know what's going to happen."

Laurel's brows raised. "Well then. I don't think I've ever heard those words uttered from your mouth before."

I snorted, despite the tone of our conversation and what we were about to do next. "At this point, we have to hope. Because nothing is going as planned. And we've been going along with Oriel's journey and his secrets for far too long. We know who he is, we might not know where he hides, but we know that he's going to come for us. And the core of the town."

"The core that is currently still wrapped around you," Ash grumbled.

I nodded tightly before I cupped his cheek. "Your dragon saved us. And the core's magic is saving me. It's not overwhelming me. I don't know how to explain it, but it feels like it was always meant to be."

"It won't always be like that," Laurel insisted. "It will overwhelm you soon. It's far too much magic for a single witch, even one of your caliber."

I swallowed hard and nodded. "I understand. I know. I don't want this magic, I just want my own, and I have it. It's just currently blending with the core of the town."

"Only the core of the town was able to transfer some of its magic to me, for Rome," Sage said as she came forward, her hand tightly clasped with Rome's. Jaxton came up from behind them and wrapped his arms around Laurel as I stepped away from her to hug Sage tightly before doing the same to Rome and going to Ash's side.

It was the six of us again, and I swallowed hard and looked at my friends. "The center of the power of the town did this. It brought us together. Maybe that's what our ancestors meant. That we were supposed to do something that we never would've expected."

"I'm grateful. Believe me, I'm fucking grateful," Rome growled, and Sage's eyes filled with tears again. "But I don't want you to burn out because of it."

I shook my head. "I won't burn out. That's not the problem here."

"If you say so. What are we going to do now?" Laurel asked.

I let out a breath, preparing myself for what was going to come next. "We're going to do what I said. We're going to do what nobody's ever done before."

"And that is?" Aspen asked as he walked forward, and he wasn't alone. Nelle was at his side, and beside her was someone I would never have thought to see on two legs again in the town of Ravenwood. Not when we had lost so much of our magic that kept *his* magic stable.

The king of the merpeople came forward, the crown on his head made of gems and coral. His wife and mate, Jaxton's mother, a hawk shifter, held his hand and smiled up at me. More merpeople were around us, as were many of the fae. It wasn't just our people but those connected to us.

"Well met," I whispered as I bowed before the king of the merpeople.

He smiled and shook his head. "None of you shall bow before me. You saved my daughter."

"I thought Aspen did that," I said softly as I looked at the fae king.

Aspen shook his head. "I wouldn't have been able to do it without any of you."

"And since I'm standing right here, know that I'm fine. I am. A little different. But I'm fine."

She was of hawk, of mer, and fae now. A tribrid in all

sense of the word. I didn't know what her future path would be, but I would do all in my power to ensure she had that path to thrive on. And that meant I needed to fight to keep Ravenwood whole. Even if it meant becoming different.

More people filled the pack circle now. Bears, wolves, Frank, more fae, and humans.

Humans and witches. Witches who held but a single drop of power. Edith, some of the bookshop workers. A few kitchen witches said they held no power, but I could feel it humming within them. Far, far diluted thanks to time and lack of belief, but they were here. They were fighting for Ravenwood just like they always had.

And now it was time for my plan to take fruition. It would be twofold, and I had to hope that we were ready. We had lost the battle before, but we would not lose the war.

I looked around at the group of people who had come to fight for this town, to take the next steps, and an overwhelming sense of urgency filled me. The powerful magic that was not my own pulsed along with my own, and I let out a shocked gasp as everybody stared at me. I frowned and squeezed Ash's hand before letting him go, swallowing hard. "I'm fine."

"You're not fine," he grumbled, but I shook my head. I would be fine because I would find a way. Even if it took longer than expected. Because everybody who needed to know what was going on did, and that meant we would use what we had for now for our advantage and hope it wasn't too much in the end.

My mate glared at me, and I knew he wanted to wrap me in cotton wool and protect me from the world. Or perhaps hide me in his dragon hoard while growling at anyone that came near him. I wanted to smile at that, but my head ached too much to do so.

"Thank you all for coming. We're here today to take back Ravenwood," I stated, and I raised my chin.

Cheers shouted in the distance as everyone circled around us, and Laurel's lips twitched. "Well, that's one way to start it."

"We are here because Oriel is trying to take this town. He broke the wards, and he's had a lot of time and a lot of dark magic to do so," Ash continued, and I smiled at him. We had both discussed what would need to happen today since sleep hadn't come to us. We'd taken care of the injured and buried those lost. We'd used magic and spells to keep those who'd died safe from becoming revenants and shades. It had taken energy, but there had been no other way.

"How are we going to do that?" the king of the mers asked. "Not that I don't trust you all. You are the strongest witches I've ever met and process kind hearts. But against necromancers? What kind of strength will you bring?"

"Dad," Nelle mumbled, her pale cheeks darkening.

Aspen was the one that spoke up. "Sir, I have a feeling we're going to see something we've never seen before." It was odd to think that Aspen was now talking to his father-in-law, but in the end, Aspen believed in us. I had to hope that we were worth that belief.

I nodded, meeting both of their gazes. "What we're going to do is something that others have asked for, and something I never thought possible. We are a town of shifters, fae, and witches."

"That's how the town was founded," Aspen added.

"You're right. It was founded with the three witches' family, with our families," I said, encompassing the coven. My friends and family stood next to me, their chins lifted. They all knew what was coming next and what sacrifices would be made. We had to make this work. No matter the cost.

I continued. "With the witches, we were able to create the wards to protect our town from outside forces and unseen eyes. We wanted to ensure that there was a place that you could walk freely and not hide who you are. We had over a hundred years of that working until time dissipated our magic." I looked at the others, at the humans that were witches, at the shame in their eyes, and I knew I needed to continue quickly. "It's not your fault. It's not anyone here's fault. Life happens. We did not have the power to create more witches because the power comes from within, and magic has changed in the centuries. We know this. We can call to the goddess, but the goddess does not give us our power. She just shows us what power we have. But we could change that."

A few of the witches' eyes widened, but nobody said anything, and they were waiting for me to continue. I let out a breath and did so.

"This town was born with the idea of more than one: a witch, a shifter, a fae. The mers were always there to aid. Through their own circumstance, they've been there for us. The hawks, the bears, even the wolves when they were here before." I looked at the five new wolves that were now part of the bear clan, and I nodded tightly. "You've come back. For a reason. We have more than one type of shifter." I swallowed hard. "And we have come to learn that more shifters have been trying to find their way here, but Oriel has stopped them."

Some of the bears growled, and Aspen narrowed his eyes.

I let out a breath, knowing I was walking a dangerous line of hope with a people who had begun to lose all of theirs. "He has used them as shades, has used their power. We will not allow that to happen again. We will become a sanctuary for those who need help again."

"How do you expect us to do that?" a dominant bear asked, and Rome growled.

Sage put her hand on his arm, and I looked at the bear alpha and nodded tightly. "It's okay. They have questions, and I'm going to give the answers that I can."

"Watch how you speak to her," he growled.

The bear lowered his gaze, but I understood it wasn't

that he wasn't allowed to ask questions. He just wasn't allowed to growl at the alpha.

"The way that this town was built was to create a core of magic. Most of you know about it, but not all." I let out a breath. "Oriel wants the core of magic for his own desires. Once he gets that, he could literally take over the world. He will have access to stores of magic hitherto unknown. We must protect that." I swallowed hard. "But the core magic is currently wrapped around me."

There were a few gasps, and Aspen's eyes widened.

I met the fae's gaze directly. "I cannot hold onto it for much longer in the capacity I am, but it kept me whole. It saved Rome. We must protect it, but I believe there's something we can finally do using the magic that was given to it by witches. We can finally pull our weight."

A few of the human witches inhaled sharply, and I smiled at them. "We can bring forth new magic to unlock the potential of power within each of you. We will not just be the coven of three. Yes, we will be the strongest to our anchors because of our training and prophecy, but we can open it, so you have the potential to find your own magic. To find the goodness within yourself. Yes, it might hurt. Yes, it is dangerous. But throughout these years, our shifters have grown stronger and have added more weight and protection to our town. The fae have grown stronger and more tightly connected. Our connections to other packs and realms have increased. But we witches have faded. We can change this. Finally, we can find a way to make us a coven in truth. Not of three, but of power, and of honesty, and of goodness. The core is telling me this can happen. The ancestors that I spoke with have pushed us here. Together, we can build wards strong enough to keep Oriel out, to bring the fight to him. And once we do this, we can protect Ravenwood for once and for all."

The others shouted and cheered, and I swallowed hard, my mouth dry. I looked at Ash, and he continued for me because, just then, I was exhausted.

Ash cleared his throat. "We will not force this upon you. It must be your choice. You will be trained over time —*after* the battle because...because I have a feeling there is something the goddess is waiting for." We couldn't be any more detailed than that, and I knew it was from the original Ravenwood, an odd sense of knowing that surprised me.

I stepped forward. "You will learn what it means to be a true witch, on top of the kitchen witch powers that you may already have and possess. You are not nothing. You are not less now than who you will be. Know that the power you have will only be amplified. It will not change who you are but enhance who you could be. It will hurt. You might find an element, you might not, but we four have the elements, and we can teach you. But today, at this moment, if you step forward, we will build a new coven, a stronger one."

Ash looked at me, and I nodded tightly before continuing. "And then we will build the wards as a group. Not of coven, but of Ravenwood. It will not be tied to just witches or to me. It will be tied to everyone who puts a step forward to protect their family, their home, and our future. If we are able to do this, we can keep Oriel out and bring the fight to him. If we can do this, I will give you everything that I have. I promise you."

Edith walked forward and gripped my hand with her bony fingers. "You have given us everything. Time and time again, we have watched you nearly fall, nearly fade because of the power within you. You have always protected us. You have watched your friends and family leave and pass because of the power you have given us as our Ravenwood. I will follow you to the end of the earth, Rowen. And if you give me the chance to touch the magic that I could have always held? I will owe you my life."

"No, you owe me nothing."

"We owe you everything. You are Ravenwood, but we are Ravenwood with you. So, I will stand and fight. I may be old, my days numbered, but I will fight with you. And it will be kind of nice to see what kind of witch I could be. Especially after all these years."

Tears fell, and I couldn't help it, as witch after witch came forward. Young girls, older boys, wrinkled men, and strong women. Every person who had ever thought they could once be a witch within the town, who had sacrificed part of themselves as humans to be here to protect others. To find a place where they felt accepted.

They walked forward, and we were not alone.

Fifty. There would be *fifty* witches. I counted them. With the coven already in place, there would be fifty witches.

And as the core of the magic pulsated within me, I knew we would be enough.

"Where do you need us?" Aspen asked softly as the witches stood in front of me, looking pale but ready.

Finally, they would be able to fight and not just try to protect the weak. They would be able to fight back. And I knew that gave us the energy to do this.

"Please, work with the shifters and the mers, and protect this circle. And then, we will come together, create the new wards, and plan to take this to Oriel. No more waiting for him."

"We will do this. Blessed be, witch."

He lifted his chin, and I lowered my head, and the king of the fae went to protect our coven, small for now, but not for long.

I looked at my coven, best friends, and mate, and I took their hands.

"Are you ready?"

"As ready as we'll ever be," Ash began. "You are bright. You are powerful. You can do this. But don't just rely on yourself. Rely on us."

"Damn straight," Laurel put in, and I laughed.

"Don't drain yourself for this. Use all of us."

"If you die because of this, we are going to haunt you," Edith called out, and I laughed, despite myself.

And so, I looked at the others and nodded tightly, and we four stood in a circle for a moment before breaking apart to stand in a line.

"Witches in front of me, stand straight with your shoulders back, chests out, palms outstretched and facing the sky. Close your eyes and focus on that kernel of magic within you."

The witches nodded tightly before they did. I could sense their fear, and trepidation, and anticipation.

It was time.

"Blessed be the witch.

Witches three foreshadowed be.

Come into the light.

For magic is not always right.

Forget thy power.

Forget thy path.

Become who you're meant to be.

Find the heart of the ancestors.

Find the heart of those lost.

Find the power within.

Become coven.

Become witch.

Become you.

So I will it, so mote it be."

Power cascaded through me, shocking through my system. I heard gasps and shouts, and some fell to their knees. Light burst in the air, but the fae did something, like a bubble of time and magic to protect us from seeing eyes. No one could see this moment but us.

For that, I was grateful to Aspen, but now I needed to focus on the witches. Laurel beamed while Ash looked like stone, ready to protect any who fell, whose magic was too much for them.

But these witches were power. They were strong. They could take this.

Sage laughed, her eyes filling with tears, as I looked over my friends and family, at my new coven. Witches of fire, of earth, of air, of water. All of the spectrum, they stood there, every single one held an element. There were shouts, as heat and sparkles and diamonds and shattering light filled the air as anchors were etched on skin. But there was no pain.

Not with the core of the magic and the ancestors themselves holding us in place.

I looked over the coven, and then past them, and saw the original Ravenwood. The original Prince. The original Christopher. They smiled at us and nodded, and I knew I had taken the right step.

"We will aid you through this battle, to bypass some training, but then you must become a true coven, to learn what we can speed through for now," my ancestor whispered, and I finally understood. The new witches would have sudden control over their powers for only a few short hours, and then they would be in need of training.

We were not coven three or four. We were the Coven of Ravenwood.

And we were finally who we were meant to be.

There were tears, little sparks of fires from fingertips, and gasps.

"It looks like we'll be training," Laurel said with a laugh as she clapped her hands. And then we moved. All of us hugging and touching and connecting to our fellow witches.

"I can't believe this," Edith said as she twirled water through her fingers. "I'm a water witch."

"And I can't wait to show you what I've learned," Sage said as she hugged her tightly.

Others smiled and held each other, and they looked at us, and we were ready. The core of the town pulled away from me slightly and settled back into itself. We didn't need it right now. It knew it. It had given what it could, and now it was resting. And I had never felt so alive.

"And now, I need you to all hold hands with whoever you see. With witch, with fae, with shifter. Mix it up, make sure there's a connection to someone you don't know, to someone that you love, to anyone. And I want you to all repeat after me. We don't have a lot of time," I said quickly, and Ash nodded.

"He's on his way," Ash whispered, his dragon in his eyes. "I can feel it."

"We're going to build the wards now?" one of the

teenage wolves asked, as he held Edith's hand with one and the mer king with the other.

"Right now. Of all species, of all lives. We are Raven-wood. We are strong. We will banish Oriel from this land, and we will fight him on our terms. We will no longer be on the defense. It is time we remember who we are." I let out a breath. "We are Ravenwood!" I called out.

"Ravenwood!" the others called back.

And it was as if a spark of magic had been ignited, a pulse of magic and energy radiated from our center.

I held Nelle's and Ash's hands, knowing I needed my mate for this, as well as the other parts of my original coven. They each held their mate's hands, and a stranger's.

We were ready.

"Repeat after me!" I called, as the wind whirled.

Because Oriel was on his way, I could hear the revenants crushing through the forest. I could feel the shades slinking through like a dark mist. Oriel was on his way, but he would not win.

Fear began to coat my tongue, and the others could sense it. But they did not back down. For we were ready.

"Dear goddess, protect us.

Strengthen our resolve, from hearth to home, from air to water. From fire to ash. From hope to dust.

Bring forth our power.

Bring forth our light.

Protect us, dear ancestors.

We are one, not of witch, not of shade.

Protect us, goddess.

For we are Ravenwood.

And we are one."

The wards snapped into place, a giant force of power and wind as it began in the center of our circle and burst out of us. Hair billowed, and someone shouted, but we all stood. Even the small bear cubs in bear form clung to their mothers were still part of our power. With the immensity of who we were, it wasn't pulling at us. It wasn't draining us of who we were. No, it was amplifying. Finally, we had solved who we needed to be. And we were one.

There was a shout, a scream, and then it was as if I could sense it and see it.

"They're beautiful," Sage whispered from behind me, and I could hear the tears in her voice.

The new wards were in place. And they were no longer connected to one. No longer connected to just the witches. They were connected to Ravenwood itself.

They would not fall again, not to darkness, not to indecision. They couldn't.

We were our future.

And it was time to end Oriel once and for all.

CHAPTER

TWENTY

Oriel

Oriel slammed the door behind him, his jaw aching. He stomped towards his workshop and threw witch hazel over his hands, his face. He looked at his reflection and scowled. Burn marks covered his skin, but he knew he'd heal those quickly.

"Those damn wards," he grumbled.

How could they be up so fast? It had taken him months to weave himself into the magic, to slowly drain the wards using Rowen's own soul. She hadn't even realized it until it was almost too late. Now, he didn't understand what was going on and he knew that if he didn't work quickly, all his years of planning and of fighting would be for naught.

Screw that. He had sacrificed everything for his birthright. And his little sister was going to have to step out of the way. If not, then he'd kill her, just like he'd always planned. At one point, he thought maybe she'd want to fight by his side, to be the Ravenwood second-in-command to help control the shifters and the magic itself. She was strong enough that she would have been a good ally, but now she was a traitor. She was nothing.

It was time for Ravenwood to truly understand who their leader was. He would get the core of the town. He would get his magic. And he would break those wards. He'd done it before. He would do it again.

The shades of those who had fought with him, who had sacrificed themselves for him, hovered around him. Faith, Renee, the hawk. They were all there. For him. He swallowed hard and pushed at his magic, pressing against the runes on his forearms. The shades strengthened, and he nodded.

Good. He was alone now. Just with his shades, his revenants. Alone.

He was the only person he could trust.

And while he couldn't trust the others, it was time to bring those who wanted magic and power of their own. Though he'd have to end them when the time came, he could use their power and numbers for now.

He would use whatever he could and everything he had gathered over the years to take what was his.

It was time Rowen Ravenwood understood exactly what happened when you fucked with the wrong man. When you took what wasn't yours.

Because the magic was his.

Only his.

He was the Ravenwood. By birthright, and by power.

And it was time to take back everything that had been stolen in the first place.

CHAPTER
TWENTY-ONE

Ash

The power beneath my claws thrummed, and I beat my wings, *once, twice,* to settle myself in the air. It had only been a week since I'd first shifted, a week since I'd regained my soul and my bond with Rowen. In some respects, it felt as if it had been a lifetime.

It had felt as though countless lifetimes had passed since I'd first set eyes on Rowen and my own power.

In the past week my life had shifted along with my body into this form, and the world had turned to chaos and mastery. I still couldn't quite believe we were only hours away from taking the battle to Oriel.

After years of waiting, it was time to face our darkness head-on and take back what was rightfully ours.

Not power. Not even the town. But our peace and right to life. That was ours in truth, and with the connections forged in a town of hardship and secrecy, we were going to fight as one.

That is, of course, if I could figure out how to land after flying for longer than thirty minutes. Easier said than done as I dove between two hawks, one being Jaxton. They flew and dove like they were practicing for an air show, and I was still somewhat clumsy in the air *and* on the ground. I was getting better, however, and that's what I needed to continually tell myself so I wouldn't be a liability on the battlefield next to Rowen.

Because I *would* be next to her.

My beautiful witch mate who held the power of the world in her hands and had freely given to those in need rather than selfishly hanging onto any power she could.

That was my witch.

And one I would freely fight and die for.

Not that I actually *wanted* to die for her. No, I had plans that included a future with both of us living. Only in the past week we'd hardly had any time to spend together, and, more than once, one of us had been unconscious thanks to a power drain or having just fought.

Tonight, once I landed and shifted, we would take some time.

Others were doing the same, and honestly, it was

something we needed, even if it might seem as though we were wasting any time we had.

Not tonight, though. Tonight, I would fly, find my mate, and prove to her exactly what we were fighting for.

The hawks on either side of me flew around me in formation, and I let out a huff of breath, smoke billowing through my nostrils. I swore I saw Jaxton's eyes narrow at me, and I held in a little smile as the hawks continued their formation and flew in for a landing. I followed suit, and thankfully this time did not fall on my face. It was only just though, and I was honestly a little worried that I would end up slamming into the ground next time. I needed to learn to use these new powers of mine for something other than being the blockade against shades. Of course, perhaps that was what I was good for. To block those who would want to harm Rowen and give her time to do what she did best.

Fight Oriel and save Ravenwood.

I landed somewhat softly, my feet digging into the ground near the aerie. Jaxton shifted and changed back into his jeans and t-shirt as I focused on the bond between my dragon and myself and shifted back into human form. He tossed my black pants and pullover to me, and I nodded my thanks. "I wish clothes would just shift with you. It would make things easier."

"True, but then my mate couldn't see my naked chest, so I figure it evens out in the end."

The beta to the hawk snorted and walked away while I

just rolled my eyes. "You do realize that your mate is my sister. And things get a little weird."

"Maybe. Although you only used to glare at me slightly before. I like the fact that you get all huffy now, Mr. Dragon With a Soul. It feels warm and happy."

I shook my head. "You're staying in tonight with Laurel then? I don't want to know what's going to go on. I assume you're going to eat cookies and drink tea by the fire while you discuss your bird ways."

"Of course. Bird ways. I could probably make a joke there, but I'm not going to. It's been a long night."

I finished dressing and slid my feet into my shoes. "I'm going to Rowen's. Not to talk about bird ways."

Jaxton snorted. "You see? You can talk about things like that, but I can't."

I narrowed my eyes, even as my lips twitched. "Because she's my sister. And frankly, Laurel will kill you for talking about shit like that."

Laurel moved forward, fake sneering. "Talking about shit like what? It better not be our sex life, Mr. Hawk."

"You know me. I can't help it." He leaned forward, kissed Laurel squarely on the mouth, and she smiled wide up at him.

My chest warmed, watching the two of them. I'd almost lost my sister. And the fact that I'd almost lost her, even while trying to sacrifice part of myself to protect her while I had no soul, nearly broke me. Because I wouldn't have reacted the way that I should have. I hadn't. I had thought she had died, same as Jaxton, and part of me hadn't been able to break through my own personal darkness to feel what I should.

And I hated myself for it.

"What's that look, big brother?" She came up to me and hugged me tight, and I kissed the top of my little sister's head.

Every time I thought about what happened to Laurel when I hadn't been truly myself, my dragon roared, and I wanted to burn something. "Nothing. Just thinking."

"Tomorrow's going to be a big day. Get some sleep. Hug your mate. I know Rowen needs rest and just a moment or two to breathe. Help her do that."

"I will. I love her. She's mine."

Laurel met my gaze. "Then make sure she knows that."

I smiled. I couldn't help it. "Of course, I will. And I'm glad that you're mine too. My family, my blood. And I'll fight beside you tomorrow. We're going to make it through this. I promise you that."

She raised a brow at me. "I'd like to hope that will be the case. You and me against the world. Just like always, or perhaps a little different."

I hugged her tightly again, then met Jaxton's gaze. "Rome and Sage are already off in their den, and I'm going to Rowen, but we'll meet tomorrow morning, and we'll fight."

"I know. And we will win. Because there's not another option."

"You're right. There isn't. But I just want you two to know that I am grateful for you. I always have been. Even when I wasn't myself, I'm grateful for your friendship, for your connections, and that you found each other."

Laurel blinked away tears and scowled at me. "Why are you making me cry? I don't know if I like it."

"I have a lot of years to make up for, Laurel. A lot of things that I regret."

"That wasn't you," she began, and I cut her off.

"No, that was me. The part of me that I hate and will always regret, but it was me. But you always held me back. You were always my conscience when I didn't have one. Thank you for being my guide and my sister. Thank you for always believing in me when the others had to push me away."

I looked at Jaxton, let out a breath. "Thank you for being there for her and for Trace." I swallowed a lump in my throat as Jaxton hugged Laurel tight to his side. "I'm sorry that I wasn't here fully to mourn him with you. But I will. I will every day of my life. He was my friend, and I lost him long before he left this world, and that's one more regret I'll have to the end of my days."

"Don't have those regrets. Just move forward and be the man that I know you are."

I smiled at them, squeezed Laurel's shoulder, then did the same to Jaxton. "I can't quite do that, but I can do some of it. Now, I'm going to go see my mate."

"Just don't let whatever you just said here be a good-bye. I don't think I would be okay if I had to say goodbye."

While Laurel glared at me, even as she cried, I left my sister and my best friend back in their home and jumped in my car to head towards Rowen's. In the past week, I hadn't set foot in my house. In the place that I had bought with money that I had made when I had had no soul. Money that meant nothing now other than perhaps being able to help others later. But that would come. First, it was Rowen. Then it was Ravenwood. I would sell my home, maybe demolish it since it was such an eyesore, far too big for a town like this, because Rowen's home would always be hers. It was of the family, so I wasn't going to force her to move out of it. If anything, I was considering begging her to let me to move in. Or maybe just do it, when she wasn't looking, of course. I would just show up and never leave.

It was the sneaky side of me that hadn't been there before I'd lost my soul, but it was there now. And I didn't mind it in the least.

I pulled into Rowen's driveway, and my eyes nearly fell out of my head when I glimpsed a very naked Rowen walking through the gardens.

Then I looked up at the moon bright in the sky and grinned.

"Oh, going to be that kind of night."

I turned off the engine and made my way to the garden, around the house, swallowing hard as I watched her walk sky-clad under the moon, her fingers playing through the roses.

She was gorgeous, her long dark hair flowing down her back, her rose-tipped breasts high and full. Her hips rounded out to a thin waist, the dark patch of curls between her legs beckoning. I'd had my mouth and my hands on every inch of the skin bared to the moon, and I would do so again if the goddess was willing.

Rowen opened her eyes, those gray eyes that beseeched me, and smiled. "Welcome home, Ash."

"Home. I was just thinking of home."

"We never spoke about it, but here right? Here's our home?"

"Damn straight," I growled, then I moved forward and cupped her face. I pressed my lips to hers, and she grinned, her nails digging into my back as she kissed me back.

"I could get used to this—you naked when I come home."

"I would assume you'd like me better with pearls on and a glass of whiskey ready for you."

"I'm not going to make a pearl necklace joke, but if you'd like just to wear the pearls and maybe some high heels, we could make do."

She shoved at me, laughing. "Gross."

I winked. "Not so gross when I'm pumping inside of you."

"Sure. Whatever you say." She waved me off even as

laughter danced in her eyes. "It is a full moon, and I was going to do some spells to try to strengthen my own resources. Normally we would do this with the coven, though with so many new witches, I thought it would be too much for all of us. And, frankly, I don't know if I'm ready to get naked in front of the entire coven."

"You don't ever do anything sky-clad in front of them."

"True, just by myself." She swallowed hard. "Or with you."

"Always."

"You're back, Ash. I never let myself think about this moment, to hope for it. But you're back, and I never want to let you go. I'm so afraid of what's going to come tomorrow, the fights that we're going to have to endure, the losses. We've already lost so much, and I don't want to do it again."

I lowered my forehead to hers and held her close, her skin against my clothing. "You are mine. Always. I will regret to the end of my days that we lost so much time to the curse. But I'm back, and I'm going to earn you."

"I wasn't perfect when you were gone. You don't have to earn me. But we have to earn the goddess's wishes. And earn her hope. So, let's do that together. No more looking into the past and regretting what we could've had and what we don't have now. Yes, we lost those years, but we have so many years in front of us if we defeat Oriel tomorrow." She pulled away, fisting her hands by her sides. "I just wish I could look into a crystal ball and figure out exactly how to do that."

She turned on me, her hands on her hips, and looked like a naked warrior goddess. I fell in love all over again.

"I feel like I should be naked for this conversation."

She raised a brow. "When we do the spells in a moment, you will be, but if you get naked right now, I'm not going to be able to think."

"I'm hard enough right now that I can't think. Just saying."

She smiled softly. "This is what we have been fighting towards my entire life. We knew from the prophecy from our ancestors long before we were born that we would have to fight the darkness. The darkness is of *my* blood, and I just can't believe it. But I should. It only makes sense. A Ravenwood created, and a Ravenwood can destroy."

I moved forward again, stripping off my shirt in the process. Her eyes widened, but I just shook my head and cupped her face, brushing my lips to hers.

"A Ravenwood did all of that, but a Ravenwood can also save. And so can a Christopher, and a bear, and a Prince, and all of the others. You are not alone. We just did a few amazing spells to prove that." I tapped the end of her nose with my forefinger. "Stop forgetting that you are not alone."

She wrapped her arms around my waist and snuggled in deep. "I'll try not to forget. Now, take off your pants."

"I thought you'd never ask."

"We're going to pull energy from the moon and ask the goddess for her blessing."

"Okay then, let's do it."

I stripped off my shoes, then my pants, and I held Rowen's hands, both of us facing each other, our eyes closed as we tilted our chins towards the moon. And I breathed in the energy of the goddess, and the magic around us, hoping it was enough.

Power radiated around us, and I looked down at my glowing mate, the woman I wanted to be my wife, mother of my children, and knew first she was warrior, coven leader of Ravenwood.

And mine.

I kissed her hard, and she wrapped her arms around my neck. I delved my tongue between her lips, both of us moaning into one another. My cock was hard between us, and as I shifted so my leg was between hers, I found she was wet, both of us ready and needing. We tumbled to the ground, all limbs and hot breaths and gasps, and then I was on my back, the dirt beneath me. I used my magic to soften the blows for her own knees as she straddled me. And the magic of air above her and earth beneath me pulsated between us, our elements coming together as we did the same. Our bond flared, and she sank her wetness over my cock and we both froze, knowing that this was a perfect moment in time for the both of us.

She slid her hands down my body, hovered over me,

her breasts falling in front of my mouth, and I grinned. I licked one nipple, then shifted to lick the other, and then we moved. She arced along me as she rode me and I pumped into her, both of us fast and needy and wet and just everything that we could ever need. Our mating bond flared, sending energy back and forth between us, and I felt the core of the town push at us, wanting to embrace us, but I shifted, pressing Rowen into the earth so she was below me, one leg up over my shoulder as I pumped into her, both of us gasping. I would not let too much power take over because we didn't need the town's core anymore. We needed to protect it. I couldn't let the vast amount of untapped power overwhelm my mate. And we both knew it. We made love, coming together as we whispered each other's names.

I breathed in her heady scent, letting the magic settle into our skin.

And as I cupped her face and looked down at her, I knew tomorrow would be the end of something. However, I didn't know what.

I knew we had to fight. And we had to win.

Because no matter the cost, our payment was coming due, therefore we had to be stronger than Oriel, smarter, but in the end, we had to fight fate.

And fight for each other.

TWENTY-TWO

Rowen

I felt as if I'd been waiting my entire life for this, but now it was finally here. We would end this war. Because we had to. I didn't want to lose any more of my friends, my family. I didn't want to lose this town. But I knew we were willing to burn Ravenwood to the ground as long as we could save its people and keep the magic out of his hands. I knew this. Everyone who resided in Ravenwood knew this. We would do our best not to let that happen. Ash came to my side then, a frown on his face, and I looked at the man that I loved, the man I knew would fight to the end with me. I could not lose him. I knew this, but I didn't think he did. I wasn't sure he understood what I would do for him. After so long of being apart, we were finally together, and part of me was truly afraid that we wouldn't get the ending we deserved.

"Why are you looking at me like that?" he asked, a brow raised. In that moment, Ash looked so much like the man he had been before, with the haughty look of a man who knew what he wanted and didn't mind the coldness within.

"I was just thinking you're so different than you were before, but I like this person. I like the man that you've become, Ash."

I swore he blushed before he shook his head, his lips twitching. "I'm learning to like the man that I've become. too. Though it's not exactly who I thought I would be that first time we were together. And neither one of us are those people anymore. I'm a blend of the man I thought I would've become and the man that I am, the man that lost everything. Then again, you're the blend of the woman you've needed to become in that time as well."

I smiled then, cupped his face. "You're right. And we're just figuring out who those people are together."

He cupped my face, pressed his lips to mine before he whispered, "And I will fight to the end of the earth to make sure we have time to find out who we are together. We fight today, but we do it side by side. We will take down Oriel. And we will do it together."

I nodded, my eyes not filling with tears. I was out of them and, frankly, I needed to be strong for this. People were waiting for us, and we would go to Oriel. We would fight because Ravenwood was ours.

"Are you ready to go?" he asked, and I nodded tightly before I turned and walked out of my home to see Laurel, Jaxton, Sage, and Rome there.

My gaze searched over Rome again, as if afraid he wasn't truly there. And when Sage gripped his hand a little tighter, I knew she was thinking about what had happened before, as well. We hadn't had a lot of time to discuss it, the fact that Rome had *died*, and it was only the core of the town that had brought him back. We would eventually try to come to terms with what happened, as he had with his brothers. But first, Oriel.

"My sisters, and brothers. We're going to fight today, and we're going to win. We have a plan. We have our magics. And we're taking the fight to Oriel."

"Damn straight we are," Rome said with a small smile, before he rolled his shoulders back. "The others are in position, and we know where to go."

We did. Oriel had been closer than any of us had ever imagined. Just on the other side of the forest surrounding my house. He had been so close to me, so close to the Ravenwood ancestral home, and none of us had known it.

He was taunting us, and I couldn't believe it. I couldn't believe how close he had been all this time, but that just meant it would be easier to take the fight to him.

"For Ravenwood," I whispered.

"For Ravenwood," the others called back.

We moved through the trees as one, the other witches filtering through, coming to our sides.

Some were young, *so young*, but they were prepared. Or at least as prepared as we could be. They knew their magics, and the goddess was with us. I had to believe. If we didn't move now, Oriel would come for us. We knew this. So, we had to move quickly.

And I had to be the first. I stepped through the wards, knowing that our new magic would protect the town and the innocents, but the fighters would be outside the town wards. To keep Oriel on his toes.

I stepped onto his land, and the scent of death surrounded me. So many dead, so many lay dying. The corpses of revenants, of those who hadn't been destroyed. And they had been here the entire time, and he had hidden them from us. Until the new magics. The magic that could protect the town, that had unveiled the inner magic within each of the witches, had shown us this. And finally, we knew what Oriel was.

"Oh, big brother, it's time to end this." I was done waiting. Done being hurt, done being attacked. Now we would fight.

Ash came through next, standing at my side. "Do you think he's too weak to come out of his little house? I think it's bigger than mine. That should tell you something. Exactly what is he missing?" His voice carried, and I held back a smile even through the nerves.

"He has to steal his magic and use dark runes in order to try to fight. So, it must not be much."

The others came through, just our small coven, the hidden witches still within the wards in the trees, watching and waiting. We would fight witch against witch, witch against revenant. And Oriel would lose. I knew it to be true, deep in my heart, even as worry laced around me.

Oriel stepped out of his house, his suit immaculate, the revenants slowly crawling out from the eaves of the house, surrounding him. "I see you found me. It really wasn't that hard, was it? I mean, it did take you a while. Far longer than I assumed. For the Ravenwood and all..." He tilted his head as he stared at me. "Something's different about you, dear sister."

I matched his tone, even as anger riled through me. "I'm ready for this to be over, brother of mine. We could've had a chance. You could've done something with yourself and tried to come here to me. We could've been true siblings, where we fought together, and we took care of this town as one. Instead, you chose the side of darkness. You etched those runes on your skin, and now you will deal with this."

"I'm tired. I'm tired of trying to pretend that I really care about what you want. You will bow before me, or you will die. There is no middle ground here."

I raised my chin, my magic competing with that of the core of the town wrapping around me. "You killed our family. You killed my friends. You've tried to take so much from us, but you will never take Ravenwood. You'll never take who we are." Tears threatened, but this time with purpose, with who I was and always had been.

"I already have, darling. And I'll take even more before the night is over."

And then he moved. Revenants poured out of the building, as well as from the farmhouse next door—hundreds of them, all under the power of one necromancer. I had never seen such darkness, such power all at once, and yet we had to defeat this. And then I realized that perhaps Oriel wasn't alone. The shades themselves were also controlling the revenants. Somehow, he had enough power to control a shade and, therefore, have them control their own revenants. The amount of control and intense power he had was staggering.

He could've been an amazing witch within Ravenwood but had chosen violence and darkness instead. And now, this was the end. Oriel held up his hands and dark smoke billowed around the field between us. It was black and purple with sparks inside, and it slithered and snaked around the revenants and came towards us.

However, Oriel thought he was alone with us. But he wasn't. He may have his shades, but we had more.

Ash looked at me once, nodded tightly, then shifted to dragon to protect us from the shades. My heart burst at the glorious side of him even as fear slid over me. I was so scared this would be the last time I saw him, the last time we fought side by side.

I wouldn't let him die.

I couldn't.

The revenants came, claws bared, and I pulled out my sword as Laurel did, using my air magic along it, slicing through the closest revenant. I fought, and I claimed, trying to get to Oriel. It had to be me. I had to be the one to get to him. I knew this. So, I moved, using Ash as my shield, and I fought my way towards Oriel. My brother stood there, a smirk on his face as he used his magic for darkness, pulling at the souls of those around him and pushing his shades towards us. Ash blocked them, spewing fire. Oriel shifted up a hand, blocking the fire from touching him, but it burned the closest shade, a young man that I didn't recognize, and I ignored the pain in my heart. Because Oriel had killed that man. Had used the shifter for horrible purposes. And hopefully, with Ash's power just then, we were able to give that man peace. I had to hope we did, or all of this was for nothing. There would be no peace for anyone.

Ash moved forward, pushing himself towards the shades, but this wasn't enough. Not yet. The other witches came from the trees, the power of our ancestors filling their veins. They had watched me, had trained, though not fully. I knew the ancestors were with us through them and were making this something that we could fight together.

The witches moved forward, going in groups as they whispered spells under their breath. But they were not alone, within each smaller sections of the coven were an earth, fire, air, and water witch, plus two shifters with each group. Either wolf, bear, jaguar, panther, or hawk. Shifters from all over, strangers who had come to town over the past months, and shifters we hadn't even known were on their way. They were protecting our witches. The witches fought the revenants, and the shifters aided. We were working as one.

That wasn't all. I saw Ash's gaze narrow, but I knew we had to keep fighting.

Ash growled, and I nearly staggered under the weight of a revenant. I jumped onto Ash's back, and he gave me a look with those dragon eyes of his, but I didn't stay for long. I slid down the other side of him, knowing that I needed to keep fighting. Ash would keep at the shades, and I would protect my mate the only way I knew how. Get to Oriel.

But then others came. And they weren't ours.

My jaw dropped as dozens of dark witches came over the ridge, all in black cloaks, all stinking of death magic, and runes.

"Did you think I was alone? Oh, I had my team, but there's more than one witch out there that wants Ravenwood. Soon they will be mine, all of them. But first, we'll work together. Something you've made us do, for now. Can you fight all of us? I don't think so, little sister. Give up now."

"Never!" I screamed. I looked over the other ridge and shouted. "Now!"

Flaming arrows burst from the trees as the fae slid out from hiding, their own magic guiling and ready for anything. The witches in dark cloaks shoved at their magic, but Aspen and the fae were strong. Far stronger than they had let us know all this time. Sparkly and sizzling magic shot out from them, and then water slammed out from beneath them, the merpeople working with them. Nelle and her mate, the king of the fae worked as one, pushing out the dark witches who thought to come at us.

Some might not be full necromancers, but they still had runes etched on their skin that told me that they had taken the darkness as their own. That they were using magic to try to get at us. So, we would fight back. We would continue to fight. Aspen and Nelle and her parents, the hawk and the king of the mers, fought, their people taking on the newcomers.

We had figured that Oriel would have more up his sleeves other than shades and revenants, and we had been right. But he hadn't known that we had so many others. And as more revenants came, at least a hundred more, I knew we would have been outnumbered, except for the fact that we had more up our sleeve as well.

"Now!" Rome growled as Ash shifted back to human, my spell that I had worked on him giving him at least pants to fight in. He winked over at me, pulling a sword from Aspen's sheath as the fae king came closer, and we fought side by side, taking down the revenants. The shades were still coming, but I knew it was taking too much out of Oriel. Sweat dotted my brother's brow, and the shades backed off as if they were recharging.

Good, it was taking time. But, at the sound of Rome's call, I knew reinforcements had arrived, and more shifters pilled out of the trees.

The Alpha of all alphas, Rome's father, poured out of the trees with his pack. Countless bears, wolves, and other shifters that were not of Ravenwood, but still kin, came forward. We had planned and scried for years for this moment, but it was only now that we could use all of our people. We'd known the darkness was coming, but not the true nature until Sage had shown.

If we'd used our people before, we wouldn't have been enough. Without the core, without witches, without knowing where my brother lay in wait or even who he was, we wouldn't be here.

We'd have lost before we'd begun.

Oriel screamed, his gaze wide with panic. Just for an instant, but I saw it.

"We are Ravenwood!" I called out. "We will fight. You have nothing, Oriel. Just dark magic, and friends that aren't friends."

The man who was of blood but nothing else shook his head, that smirk on his face. "Look what you've needed to take me out. You can't go one-on-one little sister."

I moved forward, my power waiting. "Why would I need to? I never said I was Ravenwood. It is *we*. We can take you out. I don't need to go one-on-one with you, you monster."

"Look in the mirror if you want to see a monster."

I snorted—I couldn't help it. He didn't even have the words to lash out at me. He was nothing.

The coven, our originals, fought as more shifters and our new witches came on the field of battle. Mers and hawks and fae fighting one by one. It was a melee, but we were stronger.

And we had something that he didn't, something that he wanted. We had the core of Ravenwood. I would not allow anyone that I loved to be slain today.

Countless revenants and dark witches were falling, but none of ours had fallen yet. And as the pain of the power twisted on the bonds within me, I looked at Ash, and I knew we were running out of time. I had done something, something that only Ash knew. Something that I knew he was angry at me about.

I pulled on the core of the town, and it wrapped around me, aiding the power to protect those I loved. Each individual person on our side had a shield, one they might not even recognize, but as they fought, they were protected. By fighting with each other and being on each other's sides, and protecting one another, they enhanced the core of power.

And my magic, bleeding into the core of the town,

stretching my skin as if it were far too tight, was aiding them.

We would survive this whole, but only if we took out Oriel.

Ash shifted again as shade Renee came at us, claws bared, her mate by her side. Ash roared, fire spewing from his mouth, and Renee screamed, the shade going down, then another and another. I used my sword, hacking through revenants, getting to Oriel.

Rome was in bear form, clawing through the enemy, Sage at his side, taking out one after another. Laurel was in phoenix form, flying over the others, pushing fire down at those who had come against us. Her mate was at her side, Jaxton using his talons to claw at the eyes of anyone that came near his mate or his family.

We were fighting as one, something we had trained for all of our lives. Only it wasn't enough. It wasn't enough until we got to Oriel. The core of the town pulsated, shaking my body.

Ash growled at me, shifting back to human. "Let it go. We can take care of ourselves."

I shook my head, *knowing*. "No."

"It's you alone then?" Sage asked, her eyes wide. "Don't, Rowen. Don't use the core of the town. It's too much for you. You're going to explode."

"I'm fine. We just need to get to Oriel."

"Hypocrite," Oriel spat. "You're using the core of the magic, something you won't even let me have? And look at you. You can't even control it. You're weak. You're going to explode, die from the power within, and you're going to waste it."

His words hit me, but I pushed them away, knowing there was a purpose. "No, I'm not letting you touch my people. I'm not letting you touch my town. Fuck you, Oriel. You won't have us."

"Then come at me, little sister."

"Not alone," Ash growled, and my eyes widened as I saw him behind Oriel. Oriel and I hadn't even noticed Ash slinking behind the other man. He held his magic out, the earth rising on either side of him in stone formations as it circled Oriel. Then Ash put his arm around Oriel's neck, squeezing. "Call off the others. Save those who can be saved, Oriel."

I moved forward, my air magic billowing around me as everyone else continued to fight. No one else could be part of this, just me, Ash, and Oriel. This is the way it always had to be. Even if I hadn't realized it, this was the way it had to be.

"Let go. There's still a chance."

"Never, *bitch*. Ravenwood is mine."

I looked at my brother then, and I knew he was right. There was no other ending but this. And I thought of Penelope. Of my parents. I thought of Esmeralda. Of Rome. Of Trace. Of Alden. Of all those who had died.

And there was no saving Oriel.

There had never been.

And as tears fell, I pushed out my magic, the core of the town enraging me, and I hoped the goddess would forgive me.

With one stroke of my magic, Ash holding him back, Oriel's eyes widened, his skin going pale, dark veins pulsating underneath, the runes spread, covering his skin, then, as he screamed, there was nothing.

Only the sound of roaring in my ears as the core of the town's magic echoed, intensifying to the point that I couldn't breathe. Ash dropped the corpse of the man who had threatened our lives for years without us even knowing and ran to me. I tried to tell Ash I loved him. I tried to tell the others that now that Oriel was gone. We could survive this. That Ravenwood would survive.

But I had no words. The magic that wasn't mine stretched my skin, cracking it down the sides. Light erupted from my body, and I tried to scream, but there was nothing. My knees gave out, and I fell. I only knew Ash caught me because I could closely see the horror in his eyes. I tried to reach out, I tried to do something. But it wasn't enough.

It wasn't going to be enough.

Ash

The tether between Rowen and I began to fray, one thread at a time, as if it were unspooling from itself. I screamed, the dragon within me wanting to roar. But there was no power within the dragon to bring her back. To stop this connection to the core of the town that was too much for her. I looked up at Laurel as she fell to her knees at my side. She had gotten out of her phoenix form and laid her sword to the side of ours, her eyes wide.

"What do we do?" she asked.

I looked at my sister and swallowed hard. "It's too much magic. It's so much power."

"We need to do something," Sage whispered as she gripped Rowen's hand. The bear shifter had shifted back to human and now knelt at my side, squeezing my shoulder. Jaxton was behind Laurel, and the five of us looked down at Rowen in my arms, as her eyes widened, as she tried to breathe.

I didn't know what to do.

"Use the bond," Jaxton insisted. "Try to use the bond, for now, to siphon it off. I'm not sure what to do other than that. There has to be someone that knows what to do."

"Where's Aspen? Ask him, he'll know," Sage said, tears falling down her face. "She saved us all. You both did. We can't let this happen."

I nodded tightly, then closed my eyes, focusing on the bond between Rowen and me. I felt her air magic twining around the tattered bond and felt her tears even though she wasn't moving. I held her close, siphoning off whatever magic I could, and yet everything was breaking. I couldn't focus. It was too much. How could she hold on to all this power? I could barely hold on to the little bit that I had. It was too much for her, too much for me, too much for everyone. The core of the town was unraveling out of control, and Rowen was dying.

Jagged crevices on her skin opened as even more light and magic poured out, hitting the air and slamming into the wards of the town to our right. Oriel's magic was gone, the other shifters and witches taking care of whatever revenants remained. The shades were gone. I had taken care of those myself. Those were what I could force back to their bodies, into their own realm, to protect their souls. The dark necromancers who had remained hooded, who had only fought for some semblance of power with Oriel, were now gone, all of them dead, none of them even asking for forgiveness or redemption. No, they had fought to the bitter end, and I wasn't sure what else I could do.

The power shot into me through the bond, and I staggered back. Rome came behind me and held me up. I looked at the other man, Rowen dying in my arms.

"We need to push the core of the magic back down. It's literally tearing through Rowen to get into the earth. We can't let it touch the earth completely," Aspen added as he came forward and knelt. The mer king and Rome's father stood behind Aspen; the leaders of those factions who had helped us fight. Other witches came forward, as did Frank, and people who knew us, who were our family, circled us. The revenants were taken care of, but our town wasn't complete. Our family wasn't complete.

"The magic can't go back," Rome's father added, his voice a low growl. "It's too much for the human realm. It will break it."

The mer king nodded tightly. "If this magic gets out into the human realm, it will bring forth a new generation of magic that will not be able to be hidden from the humans." The king of the mers let out a breath. "If that happens, there will be war. There was a reason all those years ago that our ancestors pushed the magic back down.

That the dragons that had once roamed this earth helped. There is a reason we have a dragon now." The king of the mers met my gaze.

Understanding hit me, even as pain ricocheted down my body, slicing into my skin. Light pierced my own body, and Sage let out a gasp as Laurel gripped my hand.

"It's killing you too," my sister whispered.

"We have to create a new protective circle for the core of magic. We have to protect it more than we already have. Not just a secret of the town, but one that builds all powers. And it doesn't rely only on her." Or me.

Aspen nodded. "It was always coming to this. Even if we didn't realize it, it was always going to come to this."

"What do we do?" I looked at Aspen. "You were there. I know you were."

The fae king smiled softly. "I was. I was the king then. I am the king now. And I will help us create better protection for this town and our people. And, hopefully, all of us will learn from our mistakes."

"I don't care about our fucking mistakes. Help me save my mate," I spat.

The others moved around us, and I saw the shifters, the witches, the fae, all of them surround us in concentric circles, exploding in an array of magic and power, as I looked down at the woman in my arms.

She opened her gaze, her mouth moving, but no words came out. I leaned down and pressed a kiss to her forehead, knowing it was my turn.

"You saved us. Now let me save you."

"Repeat after me, and then all of us will need to sacrifice something. To give part of ourselves."

I looked at Aspen. "What do you mean by that?"

"Blood," Aspen said with a sad smile. "We will need to pierce our palms and use blood magic over Rowen. She will be our focal point, but she will not be the only one connected. We will all be connected. We'll all connect. We all protect each other."

I nodded as Aspen pulled the blade off his hip and handed it to me.

"Let's go. We don't have much time." The bond was breaking. Rowen was leaving us. My mate was leaving us.

"Protect our realm. Protect our town.

Use the power of three—the power of our protections.

We are the future. We are the past. We are the mistakes. We are the truths.

Blend our powers, blend our faiths, and become one.

We are Ravenwood. We are strength.

And we are family.

For the goddess, for the future, for us."

I pierced my hand at that moment, slid the blade over my skin as the blood welled. I dropped a drop on Rowen's skin over her heart, and it disappeared as if it hadn't been there at all. The magic sucked it up as if it were thirsty, hungry. Aspen did the same, and then each of us. Laurel. Jaxton. Sage. Rome. Even the Alpha of alphas gave his blood, though he was not a Ravenwood, he was of the power of who we were. Every single person on that battle-field, who had risked their lives, sacrificed part of themselves for this town and for Rowen.

And when the world shook, the ground beneath us erupting in power, I knew. I knew this was what we had been coming for. What everything had changed for.

"Ash," Rowen whispered as she reached up and cupped my face. I leaned down and kissed her forehead again as the core of Ravenwood settled and became what it always had meant to be.

A sanctuary for those of magical power, a place of protection. Of family. And as I kissed my mate, and the others cheered, the final echoes of battle disappearing into the wind, I whispered to my mate.

"We won."

"Ravenwood won."

And I smiled, knowing this was only the beginning, but a beginning of peace. After years of darkness, of prophecy, of sacrifice, we were home.

This was our home.

Rowen

In the two weeks since the battle, it still didn't feel real. It would take years to process all that had happened, and yet, I could only try to come to terms with where we were versus where we had begun. I sat in my workshop, surrounded by my friends, and smiled.

"What's with that smile?" Laurel asked as she sipped her wine. "Just as long as you're not thinking dirty thoughts about my brother. That's a little too much."

I laughed. I couldn't help it. "I'm just thinking about how we're sitting in this workshop of mine, not protecting the wards, not trying to break a curse, just sitting and drinking wine, eating cheese, and enjoying ourselves."

"It is a change of pace," Sage whispered as she looked over a spell book. Just for fun, for her craft. For her power. Not to fight a dark witch. It was different for sure, and I relished in it.

"So, are we ready for the large coven meeting we're about to have?" Laurel asked as she put her feet up on the workbench.

I didn't chide my sister for that. I couldn't. Not when I was just glad everyone had made it out. At least in this final battle.

The war itself had nearly cost us everything, but it had been worth it in the end. And when I broke down with Ash at night, trying to come to terms of what we'd lost, that was what I told myself.

"Hopefully, we can fit everyone in here," I said, pushing thoughts of how far we'd come out of my mind, as I looked around with a frown. "I don't know how my grandparents and great-grandparents fit their covens inside their home."

"And they didn't even have this workshop. I guess we're going to have to invest in some more chairs." Laurel looked around, her face beaming. She looked so much younger, so much happier. I couldn't help but smile.

Sage leaned forward. "We have so many new witches that want to learn their power, beyond what the ancestors gave them on battlefields."

I nodded. "That the ancestors could gift us with the knowledge on the battlefield was something I never thought possible. But now we all have to learn once again how to use our craft, and not just what was inherent that day."

Thanks to the spell used, the witches on the field had been able to fight like they had been trained for years rather than only the few small spells they had known beforehand. The ancestors could help for that short time period, but now that it had dissipated, the battle long over, the new witches were starting from scratch. "It'll be odd to have the coven of more than one."

Sage flicked water at me, the magic dancing in the air. "You've been a coven of more than one for far longer than the two weeks since the battle, young lady."

I sipped my drink and looked at my friends, my family. My sisters. "You're right. It's odd not to be alone, as I had resigned myself to thinking I would be. But I'm not. I have you. I have Ash. I have this town. And we're rebuilding. Slowly, piece by piece, we're rebuilding."

Laurel leaned forward and set her wine glass on the table. "The town is more than bricks and mortar. Yes, we're rebuilding the buildings and strengthening what we have, but we pulled through together. All magical creatures, *everybody*. We are a town that protects ourselves, protects who we love, and we always have been. And now we're ensuring that it's the case always."

I looked over at Sage, then at Laurel, and smiled. "I

guess we should get ready for the coven meeting. And I suppose Sage should tell us why she's drinking water and not wine in her wine glass. I know a spell when I see it."

Sage blushed, and Laurel threw her hands up in the air and screamed. "Oh my gosh. You're pregnant?"

Sage ducked her head, and we all stood, hugging one another. "It's early yet, but I can feel it. Rome and I are having a baby."

I kissed the top of her head, then Laurel's cheek. "And if I'm not mistaken, it seems that the bear line runs true."

Sage blinked and laughed as Laurel frowned for a minute before she snorted. "Triplets?"

Sage shook her head, then walked back slightly, putting her hand over the small swell of her stomach that was only just now noticeable. It was as if Sage's magic had hidden it from view until the time was right. "It seems that Rome's DNA is through and through. Triplets for sure."

Her eyes watered, and Laurel wiped away tears. "Trace would have been an amazing uncle. Alden, too, if he hadn't been warped in the end, but these babies are going to have so many amazing aunts and uncles, they're not going to know what to do with themselves."

"I'm so blessed. Honestly, I never thought my life would be like this—this way. But I'm so blessed to have you all in my life. Thank you for taking me in as your family. From that day when I first drove into this town, not knowing what was coming, not knowing the darkness. Thank you for taking me in. For being my family."

"On that note, thank you for saving me," Laurel said with a shrug. "For never giving up on me, even when I gave up on myself." She looked at me then, the tears in her eyes matching mine.

I swallowed hard. "Thank you for being my sisters. For reminding me I didn't have to do this alone."

"And now I'm a blubbery mess," Sage replied with a laugh, as we hugged each other and cried, and I leaned into my sisters, and I knew this was only the beginning. I hadn't expected this moment in time.

Honestly, I hadn't allowed myself to think about what would happen once we defeated the darkness. All I had been focusing on was protection and defeating Oriel. He was gone, as were his revenants and shades. The only thing left were the scars that we held inside, but now that we had worked together as a town, instead of just one person, instead of the prophecy that required sacrifice of a whole, we had come together. And that meant that no matter what scars we held, we could heal because of each other.

And soon, we would have a coven meeting, with more than just the three. Ash would be here, and I would hold onto my mate, and we would start a new beginning.

I was the Ravenwood. The coven leader of the most powerful witches in the world.

But I was not alone.

Finally, I was not alone.

CHAPTER
TWENTY-FIVE

Ash

Although Sage and Rome had already had a quiet mating ceremony, the same with Laurel and Jaxton, things were different with a new town and a new life. Our town and family needed something to cement our purpose in change and hope.

The darkness was gone, the threat eliminated. We were *safe*. That meant, somehow, I had agreed to a joint mating ceremony celebration with the six of us.

I looked at my friends and shook my head. It had been months since the attack. The town had begun to rebuild, structures no longer in ash and smoke, but new with a touch of old. We'd used magic to rebuild some of the structures so the human world wouldn't be aware, but much of it had been done from the sweat and tears of the town itself.

We were all here, finding our way. The town had wanted a celebration to remember what we had fought for. And although we could have done anything, the town had wanted the six of us to have a party like no other. So, I stood in a suit, knowing that we were still facing decisions and consequences of the choices we had made in the past. I was never going to be the man that I once was. I was always going to have to face the decisions I had made when I had no soul.

My soul was here now, as was my mate. She wore a long dark-blue dress that showcased her curves and was cut low down her chest. It made my mouth water, and I couldn't wait to strip her out of it or let her keep it on as I rucked it up her hips and fucked her slowly. From the way that she narrowed her gaze at me across the field, I had a feeling she knew what I was thinking.

Sage wore a purple gown that billowed over her growing baby bump. The fact that she was growing triplets in there scared me. However, I couldn't wait to meet the new babies. To meet the next generation of bears and witches. The next generation of Ravenwood.

Nelle and Aspen stood next to Jaxton and Laurel, my sister in a long red flowing gown. She had her hand over her stomach, her small bump only just now visible to everyone else. I held back a smile, knowing that this was something that we had never thought possible.

I had thought I was going to lose my sister long before this, and here she was, at her mating ceremony, and with child.

She was scared, as were all of us, but the Christopher curse was broken. Finally, the curse was broken.

Rome's father came up next to me and I smiled at him. "Thank you for presiding over the ceremony."

"Well, I thought I could help where I could. I've never worked a ceremony with so many other shifters that that aren't bears. And, frankly, overseeing the mating ceremony of a dragon is something that I can't wait to boast about over drinks."

I laughed. I couldn't help myself. "We like to be unique here in Ravenwood."

"I know. I miss this town. You were always so welcoming to me. Now, though, this is Rome's place—always has been. He's a good alpha."

"I would say the *best*, but you are standing right next to me," I said with a raised brow.

The other man laughed, then squeezed my shoulder. "I only wish that all three of my sons were here, but maybe they are, in some way. Watching over us."

My throat tightened and I swallowed hard, thinking of all we'd lost over the years. "You know they will be. Even with their choices, that perhaps weren't even of their own making, they're here. Watching."

The other man smiled softly before he walked away to speak with Nelle's father. The two kings in their own way had formed a bond over the battle, and I knew more connections would be made with shifters all around the world because of Ravenwood.

Nelle leaned into Aspen and grinned up at him. Her eyes sparkled magenta for a moment before going back to their normal gray, and I smiled. She was not fae, nor mer, nor hawk. She was of all three, and I knew her powers would only grow with time. Again, something else unique for the town.

Frank walked past me and grinned before he went back to talk with the three wolf triplets, a baby bear triplet in his arms. That one was sleeping, the other two in their mama's arms on the other side of the field. Ariel, the bear beta, was heavily pregnant and sitting as she watched her own cubs play around with others. There were more witches around than ever, and they and everyone else, mingled as if this is what we had been fighting for all this time.

And I still couldn't quite believe that this was where we were.

Rowen came up to me then and cupped my face. "Are you ready?" she asked, her tone full of love and warmth. It settled over me like a second skin and my dragon rumbled in happiness.

I leaned down and kissed her softly. "I suppose it is time. Rome's father has been waiting for this day for a while now."

She laughed, and then she went to her tiptoes and kissed me again. "There's something you should know before we begin."

I looked down into those gray eyes of hers and felt along the bond, her soul, her love for me, of a future that we'd almost lost before it had even begun.

"What is it?" In answer, she placed my hand over her belly. My eyes widened, my knees going weak. "Are you serious?" I whispered, knowing that others were watching us, but they wouldn't know what we were saying.

"Apparently, magic works in a mysterious way, and they wanted to ensure that the next generation of Ravenwood was whole and happy."

I threw my head back and laughed, and then I leaned down and kissed my mate hard on the mouth as others cheered and magic billowed into the air.

I picked up Rowen, twirled her around the field before we all stood in front of Rome's father. We were laughing, holding each other, standing side by side, the six of us, the original coven. And as we stood under the goddess, the ancestors watching, we celebrated Ravenwood. And ourselves.

For I had married and mated the Ravenwood. Not the last of her line. No, she was our future. My future.

And this was our beginning.

***

Want more magic, shifters, and Fated Mates?
Read Etched in Honor, the start of the Aspen Pack series!

A NOTE FROM CARRIE ANN RYAN

Thank you so much for reading **EVERNIGHT UNELASHED!**

I love writing paranormal romance and a few friends of mine have been betting the universe for witches, covens, and girl power books and that is what sparked the idea of the town of Ravenwood. I love this series so much!

While the series is complete...for now... my next paranormal series is the Aspen Pack series, beginning with Etched in Honor! Fated mates, magic, shifters, and all the heat!

The Ravenwood Coven Series:
Book 1: Dawn Unearthed
Book 2: Dusk Unveiled
Book 3: Evernight Unleashed

In the mood for more fated mates? Try the Aspen Pack series!

The Aspen Pack Series:

Book 1: Etched in Honor

The Talon Pack:

Book 1: Tattered Loyalties

Book 2: An Alpha's Choice

Book 3: Mated in Mist

Book 4: Wolf Betrayed

Book 5: Fractured Silence

Book 6: Destiny Disgraced

Book 7: Eternal Mourning

Book 8: Strength Enduring

Book 9: Forever Broken

Book 10: Mated in Darkness

If you want to make sure you know what's coming next from me, you can sign up for my newsletter at www.CarrieAnnRyan.com; follow me on twitter at @CarrieAnnRyan, or like my Facebook page. I also have a Facebook Fan Club where we have trivia, chats, and other goodies. You guys are the reason I get to do what I do and I thank you.

Make sure you're signed up for my MAILING LIST so you can know when the next releases are available as well as find giveaways and FREE READS.

Happy Reading!

ABOUT THE AUTHOR

Carrie Ann Ryan is the New York Times and USA Today bestselling author of contemporary, paranormal, and young adult romance. Her works include the Montgomery Ink, Redwood Pack, Fractured Connections, and Elements of Five series, which have sold over 3.0 million books worldwide. She started writing while in graduate school for her advanced degree in chemistry and hasn't stopped since. Carrie Ann has written over seventy-five novels and novellas with more in the works. When she's not losing herself in her emotional and action-packed worlds, she's reading as much as she can while wrangling her clowder of cats who have more followers than she does.

www.CarrieAnnRyan.com